THE
NORMIE
NEXT
DOOR

THE NORMIE NEXT DOOR

MAGNOLIA MOONE MYSTERIES
BOOK 0.5

SABRINA DUVAL

Ballydoon
Books

CONTENTS

Ballydoon Books

PO Box 1033

Oxley QLD 4075

Australia

https://louisaduval.com | hello@louisaduval.com

Third edition – ebook, paperback and hardcover duet

'The Normie Next Door' was first published in 2024 in the 'The Love Hexperts' anthology in paperback and ebook.

This novel is entirely a work of fiction. The names, characters and incidents portrayed in it are the work of the author's imagination, or used fictitiously. Any resemblance to actual persons, living or dead, events or localities is entirely coincidental.

ISBN 978-1-7637112-7-3 – hardcover

ISBN 978-1-7642311-1-4 - paperback

READER NOTE

This story uses US English and the authors have opted for US terms for common things. So you'll see neighbor, not neighbour. Color, not colour. If we got anything wrong, I apologize.

I mention a metal band called 'King's Helm'. It's fake but would have been at home at the very real Northwest Terror Fest held in 2022, as mentioned in this story.

Also, Jacob's Ladder flowers are very real and are native to Washington State. They don't look like—*ahem*—a Jacob's Ladder in terms of piercings. Look it up online, they're pretty. The piercings and the flowers 😉

CHAPTER
ONE

P rim believed good things came in threes but today, she had her doubts.

Like her coven with her sisters, for example. That was very good. And how the local bakery sold three hot cinnamon donuts for four dollars as a daily deal. And scoops of ice-cream in a cup (strawberry, chocolate and vanilla, the classic triad of creamy icy goodness).

But the three text messages from her high school nemesis, Monica Halligan, felt more like a harbinger of doom.

> Mon: Hiiii there! Can you believe it's twenty years since we 'shoot to score in 04!'??

> Mon: the twenty year reunion is on the night of Halloween and I found you were on the organizing committee for the Monster Mash Ball.

> Mon: Wouldn't it be blast if we got the Class of 04 back to Cascade High?!?! Message me and we can meet up to discuss xx

To add to her woes coming in threes, Prim had received Monica's exuberant messages during her meeting with three auditors of the High Council of Mages and Magic Users over her arrangements for the annual conference, CovenFest.

Monica's messages interrupted her explanation for increased security costs for the annual conference, and she had to stammer an apology for her phone. But, the auditors had decided Monica's proposal to have normies celebrate their twenty year high school reunion at the same event where witches and warlocks, sorcerers and spellcasters would party at the Monster Mash Ball on Halloween, was a *good* thing.

In Prim's opinion, magic and normies should not mix. Nor magic and spreadsheets, she thought, hefting her conference folder on her hip, full of last minute lists and conference administrivia.

"I feel like a boiled owl," Primrose Moone whined, breezing into the kitchen of Witches Brew, where her sisters, Geri and Magnolia, were plating up pork knuckle for customers.

"And how exactly, pray tell, does that feel?" Magnolia asked, smirking as she poured gravy over three plates.

"The auditors came to the CovenFest committee meeting." Prim threw her conference folder, notepad and committee minutes onto the stainless steel prep bench. "It was grueling and intense."

"They ruffle your feathers?" Geri balanced four plates of pork knuckle to the kitchen door. "Didn't think anything could ruffle our Prim."

Prim straightened. "This boiled owl survived. Even thrived under adversity." Geri grinned and then exited to the bar to deliver the meals. Prim darted a glance to Magnolia. "There were many questions over increased costs for security but I insisted it was necessary since your car accident last year and—"

"It will be fine. I'm fine. Truly."

Magnolia lost her powers on winter solstice last year and ever since, the Moone sisters with their aunties, and Uncle Vinnie, had tried everything they knew to figure out how to get them back, suspecting foul play.

But here they were, eleven days out from Halloween, and only days away from CovenFest opening here in Leavenworth, with no clues how Magnolia had lost her powers, or clues as to how they were taken, or indeed, no clues whatsoever about what had happened, and subsequently, no idea how to restore them.

But the witches were coming to town, and with them, knowledge.

"There's a Romanian witch coming this year who promises me she has fresh ideas about your lost powers. And Aunt Aspidistra—"

Magnolia held up a hand. "Don't remind me about Aunt Aspy. She's sending multiple messages every day via the crystal ball about preparing for some rituals that she'd like to try." Magnolia shuddered. "She wants me to drink a potion made of slime mold, bog weed from a stagnant pool under a waning moon and three drops of toad's blood."

Prim's jaw ticked. "Are we resorting to Disney level magic now? I'd imagine that in Snow White, or Sleeping Beauty."

Magnolia shrugged, shoving more pork knuckle plates through the serving hatch to Geri on the other side.

"She's exploring hearth magic. Gone full on cottagecore."

"More like swamp witch gone full on Shrek."

"You!" Aunt Aggie swept into the kitchen carrying a cheese grater in each hand. "Are you here to help? It's pumping out there and we need more hands on the bar."

"I'm not here." Prim collected her folder and committee things quickly. "You never saw me. I have to see Ray next door

3

about the Wassailing tomorrow night. I haven't heard from him."

Aggie's face softened. "Everything okay for the Wassailing?"

Truthfully, Prim found herself in a bind. Being asked by the committee to organize a traditional Wassailing normally held on the twelfth night of Christmas in January had seemed doable months ago. Several of the CovenFest delegates were arriving today and tomorrow and were curious about how Prim performed a Wassailing, a largely English ritual to scare the evil spirits from her apple orchard each year to ensure a good harvest.

Tomorrow was World Apple Day and while a relatively modern invention of an international day created in the 1990s, the committee thought it was auspicious for Prim to host a mixer in the orchard after reenacting the old fertility ritual of drinking new cider out of a wooden bowl in the oldest tree of the orchard with the King of the Orchard and chasing away goblins and imps.

A kiss was involved, too. For a man in his seventies, next door neighbor Raymond Fitzgerald managed to scale the apple tree in his backyard every year wearing his antler crown fashioned from shed deer antlers and a brass circlet that Prim's late father had made years before she had been born. When they had drunk from the first press of cider, Ray gave Prim a peck on the cheek and anyone present cheered.

If Ray had any clue Prim was a witch, along with her sisters, aunts, and her late parents, he'd never said a thing over the decades they'd been neighbors.

Ray genuinely seemed to love being a part of the Wassailing tradition that had been handed down through Prim's family for generations and continued since settling in rural Washington over a century ago.

Prim sighed. "It's all good to go. Sort of." Who needed sleep? "Just need to check in with Ray that he's okay for us to meet in his backyard for the Wassailing in his tree. He hasn't replied to my emails last week, or the week before that."

"Ray?" Aggie began vigorously grating *Emmentaler*, the traditional German cheese used to make Cheese Spaetzle, the German version of mac and cheese, and the tastier version, too, in Prim's opinion. "He's had his knees done. Just got out of hospital. Hasn't been up and about this last week. Saw Noah helping him into his wheelchair yesterday."

Prim's hand paused on the way to her mouth, full of swiped *Emmentaler*. "Noah? What?"

She didn't like the way her heart tripped a beat at the mention of his name.

Twenty years since high school and she was still acting like she had a crush on the basketball captain and Homecoming King of the Class of 2004, Noah Fitzgerald.

Crush? *Bleugh*. More like … seething disgust. Yeah, that. Definitely that.

"Such a lovely boy. I said a quick hello before I had to leave. He's looking fine, as he always did." Aggie cut a glance Prim's way. "If you stay any longer, I'm putting you in an apron to take drink orders at the bar."

While her sisters and Aggie were in Witches Brew uniforms that combined striped stockings with traditional German folk outfits, Prim was dressed head to toe in black, from velvet corset, full-length skirt, boots and coat, with her black long hair in two plaits.

Oktoberfest was in full swing in Leavenworth and Witches Brew was full of normie tourists in town for 'authentic German hospitality'. When Leavenworth reinvented itself as 'little Bavaria' in apple growing Washington state in the sixties, tourists flocked here for microbreweries with beer and cider, and the German facades of Front Street.

"I'm going, I'm going. I'll be back for close to help clean up; I promise." Prim stifled a yawn. Sleep was overrated. She could sleep when CovenFest and Oktoberfest were over on the first of November.

Aggie assured her that she looked fine, and then a chorus of good-byes and Geri yelling 'slay Goth Queen!' followed Prim out the back door and into the alleyway.

She threw her conference folder into the truck's passenger seat and turned over the engine, pulling her black duffel coat closer around her to ward off the chill after the warmth of the kitchen and out into the frigid October early evening.

Prim wasn't shivering about the chance of seeing Noah again.

No. She was cold and that was that.

She pressed down on the accelerator and headed out of town, away from drunken tourists and buskers playing *oompah* music enthusiastically on tubas on Front Street and headed towards her orchard.

TWENTY MINUTES LATER, Prim braked sharply in the driveway of her neighbor.

Three more messages had arrived on her phone.

The irony that it was *three* messages wasn't lost on Prim.

> Miri: Hi, I'm Miri. Got your details from the CovenFest brochure and wow, have to say you are a hexpert alright! Haha. What you did to that hedge fund was inspired and I need that fury to rain down on my ex's ass.

Prim's mouth twitched. That was the best of her curse

6

work to date. Bringing down corporate dude bros who had ripped off several charities had felt good. Collapsing a hedge fund without being caught was the subject of her CovenFest talk this year.

Maybe magic and spreadsheets did mix when used for revenge and justice.

> Miri: I have money, or if you take payment in other ways, I'm willing to talk terms. I want to see that wretched man turned into the slimy toad he is.

> Miri: And, if you're free over CovenFest, be great to catch up over a drink 😉

"Toads aren't that bad," Prim whispered in the dark of her truck. But the thought of cursing a warlock who had done Miri, a former lover of hers, a witchy wrong? Tempting.

More than tempting. *Fun.*

Been a while since Prim had had fun. Like a date or even any sexy fun.

Hmm, Miri's texts were more than tempting. Maybe Prim could have her fun and organize a conference, too.

Ray's porch light flicked on, and she slipped her phone into her skirt pocket, and Miri out of her mind. Hex and ex business would come later. Time to get her Wassailing in order.

She approached the front door, smiling, but that quickly faded as the door opened, a tall silhouette blocking the light from the lounge room beyond.

"Well, alright now," a deep voice said in the twilight of early evening. "If it isn't Primrose Moone."

That voice. Prim's boot caught on the top stair, and she stumbled. The night air moved; a frisson that wasn't just the chill of winter on its way or the warm air from the lounge spilling out onto the porch. That voice was like hot cocoa with a dusting of cinnamon and nutmeg, and a shot of whiskey. Like mulled wine by a log fire on a cold night.

The man moved out onto the porch, the light cutting sharply across his features.

Noah Fitzgerald. His dark grey business shirt was rolled up to his elbows and she couldn't help staring at his bare arms covered in tattoos. Tattoos he hadn't had last time she'd seen him about three years ago.

And his clothes. He wore dress pants and a button down with his hair cut long and swept up in a bun, revealing an undercut. Skull rings adorned his fingers and leather bracelets cuffed his wrists.

The Homecoming King of 2004 had transformed from letter jackets and basketball gear into skull rings and tattoos juxtaposed with formal business wear.

But he was still all smiles, those dimples on show, just like the Noah she remembered from high school.

The normie next door had rendered her speechless.

"Sure is good to see you again, Prim," Noah said, swallowing hard.

Prim double-blinked. "It is?"

Noah chuckled, scratching the scruff on his chin.

His eyes swept down and up, taking in her clothing choices, and finally settling his gaze on her eyes.

"Why are you looking at me like that? Do I have something on my face?" Prim frantically wiped her cheeks, and then her nose. "Aunt Aggie said I didn't have dirt on my face before I came over."

"There's no dirt. You look great. I mean, fine." Noah cleared his throat. "It's good to see you, Prim," he repeated. "Been ages. Years."

"You left." Her tone sounded accusatory, weirdly. Prim lowered her eyes to the decking boards. "To Seattle, I mean. You left to go to Seattle to play basketball."

"For two years." Noah shrugged. "Broke my leg. Sucked when you are on a basketball scholarship. Couldn't play anymore. Not professionally anyway."

"Oh, I remember that." Prim looked up, frowning.

And then her gaze slid up and down his body, looking at him with such an intensity as if to see right through his clothes to inspect his healed bones.

She ripped her gaze from his thighs and found Noah blushing.

"You have tattoos," she blurted.

"Huh." He smirked and held up both arms, pretending to notice his full sleeve tatts for the first time. "Will you look at that?"

A crow settled on the fence post near them and made a sound not unlike cackling. Prim's familiar, Dougie, was enjoying himself.

"You used to have a crow as a pet," Noah piped up.

"Still do." She shrugged. "That's Dougie."

Dougie huffed and then cawed. "Pet? I am *not* a pet!"

Prim rolled her eyes as Noah shook his head. "Fascinating, it's like it's talking to you. Understands what you say."

Normies couldn't understand Dougie when he spoke. To Noah, Dougie was just a normal crow, albeit a tame one that Prim cared for, making crow noises on his porch.

"He does," Prim sighed. *Too much sighing.*

"I am a demon of great power, and take my role of your familiar very seriously, witch!" Dougie shook his feathers. "Pet, indeed."

Prim huffed. "I'll give you extra treats tonight, you grumpy bird."

Noah glanced back and forth between Prim and her cantankerous familiar. Dougie cawed again but looked pleased at the idea of treats.

"Your pet matches your aesthetic."

She tilted her head. "You're making fun of me."

"I'm not, I promise." Noah swallowed hard; the pink of his

10

cheeks visible under the porch light. "Just a dumb joke. It's really great to see you again."

"Why?"

"Ah, Pops always talked about how helpful and kind you are, always offering to help him with the orchard, bringing meals over, visiting to have tea and chat."

Prim made an effort to try to soften her expression, his compliment throwing her. Her aesthetic? Had he been making a cutting remark about how she looked?

"I like your father." Her words came out defensive.

Urgh, this reunion was frostier than Santa's outhouse at the North Pole.

At school, she was known as the Ice Queen but some of the cheerleaders had a special name for her.

"You meant Dougie matches my Queen of the Damned look."

She'd walked the halls expressionless, with a glare that could reduce a grown man to a cowering idiot. She'd done so with her Biology teacher, citing a mistake in the textbook and had him apologizing profusely for setting an inferior text for the class.

And then Noah did what she did not expect. He laughed.

"Good one."

She blinked.

"You were never the Queen of the Damned at high school, even if the cheerleaders called you that."

Prim reeled, unable to parse this revelation. So many kids had openly called her that name that she made it her own.

"They just never saw you like I did."

"How did you see me?" she asked, her voice a hushed whisper.

Noah leaned forward, smirking. "A prankster."

Her mouth fell open. Whatever she expected him to say, it wasn't that.

Noah pointed a finger playfully at her, almost booping her nose. "I know it was you who pulled that stunt on Monica's locker."

She pulled back. That had been quite memorable. Monica, head cheerleader and Prim's locker neighbor, had found weird purple mushrooms growing inside her locker. The principal had given into Monica's demands and found her an empty locker beside Noah's. By the time the janitor came to remove the phosphorescent fungi, it had mysteriously vanished, and the poor man extricated Monica's books and personal effects and was treated like her personal butler moving her to beside Noah's.

"I can remember clear as yesterday how you locked eyes with me across the crowd gathered to witness Monica's purple, slimy locker and you grinned. I know you did it. Damned if I know how you pulled that off, but it's a core memory of high school."

"I—don't remember sharing a look?"

Noah chuckled again and damn it, Prim couldn't help noticing how musical his laugh sounded.

"The Ice Queen Next Door never gave me a second look after that. You never cared for the jocks. Never cared for anything other than plants, your apple orchard and up-to-date biology textbooks. And her pet."

She outright stared as Noah grinned back. His eyes danced.

Was he ... *flirting* with her?!

Dougie huffed.

Prim swallowed hard and tore her eyes from his and her gaze caught on a tattoo on his arm.

"Like the dragon?" Noah pulled up his rolled-up sleeve higher to show the full tattoo of a dragon breathing fire down his right arm. "A band in Seattle had the design trademarked and available through a couple of tattoo artists, and I treated myself for my thirtieth-sixth birthday."

She couldn't help but openly gape in silence at his tattoo.

Noah cleared his throat. "You don't want to know about—"

"King's Helm," Prim blurted, placing her hand over the dragon. "I love that band."

"Yeah, it's King's Helm all right." Noah's voice had dropped an octave, like he'd stroked each word over velvet. "You listen to them?"

Prim's mouth fell open, and she shut it again. He knew her favorite band? "They played Northwest Terror Fest two years ago. Fantastic show."

"I was there, too. They were sensational. Got the tatt later that night."

"They really were! I didn't get a tatt though."

Never in her wildest teenage dreams did Prim think she'd ever be talking to Noah about a shared and avid interest in music. He'd been the sports jock playing generic rock music over the fence.

She frowned. Hadn't he? Prim couldn't recall any time she really knew what music he'd been into, now that she thought about it.

Noah's grin widened. "Do you have any tattoos?"

Prim withdrew her hand from his arm. That touch had felt like she'd been scorched by a hot stove.

"I—um. No. Insurance!" Prim inhaled sharply to gather her wits that were now strewn across the front porch. "I need insurance details and a king of the orchard for the Wassailing tomorrow. Or I have to cancel."

Shit. What if Ray was really sick, or worse?

"I mean, how is Ray? Is he okay? I hadn't heard—"

"Rosie, dear!"

Noah's father was at the front door in a wheelchair, with one knee bandaged up and straight and his other leg bent, but the scars from his first lot of knee surgery visible.

Prim beamed, relieved and happy to see him. "How was surgery? Are you okay?"

"I am, thank you. Aren't you a sight for old, tired eyes? You look very pretty tonight, young Prim."

Ray always flirted. Always had a twinkle in his eye. There was nothing creepy or inappropriate about Ray. Always had a compliment ready for her.

"You're blushing," Noah blurted, staring incredulously like she'd spouted a second head.

Dougie cackled.

Prim straightened, schooling her features to neutral. "I am not."

"You are," he insisted. "I've never seen you blush before."

"It's the porch light," she retorted, bringing a hand to her hot cheek.

Ray chuckled from the doorway and Noah rounded on him. "You're incorrigible."

"Incorrigible!" Ray hooted. "Fancy that, hey Rosie?"

Noah huffed. "I'll do it. Be your King. Of the Orchard. For your … wazzay—I mean your was—?"

Dougie cawed, cutting him off. "He can't even say it properly. He's not a worthy king," he drawled, tilting his head as if judging him for his awful attempt to pronounce Wassailing.

Noah cut a glance back at Dougie, as if he knew what he'd just said.

"Wassailing," Prim said curtly.

"Right." He cleared his throat. "Of course. Wassailing. I can do it."

"Good work, Noah. I'm sure you're a worthy stand-in for me," his father said from the doorway. Prim blanched for a second that Ray had perfectly understood Dougie and then shook her head.

"And I saw your email just now, Rosie," Ray added. "I'll send you the insurance details before this one gets me to bed tonight."

"Thank you, Ray." Prim began to head down the stairs.

"Do you need anything else?" Noah asked. "What about my number? Just in case?"

He whipped out his phone, ready, and then it pinged, and they both automatically glanced at the screen.

> Monica: Hey there, long time no see! Great to catch up today. Would love to see you again. XX

Prim glared at Monica's enthusiastic message. The rose bush with its thorny branches swayed towards her. The old sycamore tree in the Fitzgerald's front yard shook its bare branches.

"I ran into her at the grocery store," Noah said, swiping the message away. "Wow, swear the temperature suddenly dropped several degrees right then."

Prim inhaled a deep breath, and then her phone also pinged with several incoming messages.

The sycamore tree and the rose bush both became still again.

"I have to get back to Witches Brew."

"Can I give you my number?" he asked again, his eyes big and liquid and pleading, like a cat begging for more food. "Please?"

No, he was more like a black labrador than a cat. If he had a tail he'd be wagging it, whimpering, and using his please eyes on her.

And she'd probably give him a big scratch behind his ears and call him a good boy.

Dougie laughed in his cackling way and Prim sniffed. "Fine. Here."

She handed over her phone and he quickly entered his number, sending himself a text, and Prim found herself watching his lips silently repeat his phone number. He had a full and lush mouth and she was totally sprung when he looked back up.

Prim quickly offered a quick goodbye to Ray and took her phone back and hurried to her truck.

He'd sent her a one-worded text.

> Noah: Hey

She saved his number and then drove off. In the rearview mirror, Noah was still on the porch watching her leave.

By the time she halted at the driveway entrance to wait for two cars to pass, her phone beeped with a message.

Prim glanced at her phone and butterflies took flight in her stomach.

> Noah: Great to see you again, Primrose. Looking forward to being your King

PRIM STRODE into Witches Brew and Geri met her halfway across the dining room.

"He can't be crowned King of the orchard," Prim muttered under her breath, clutching her conference folder to her chest

Geri blinked. "We'll circle back to that interesting

comment right after we deal with your guest. Did you get Magnolia's messages?"

"I did." *Another group of three*, Prim thought miserably.

> Mags: there's a Monica Halligan here asking for you

> Mags: it's been a while but is she the Monica from high school?

> Mags: omg she is the Monica from high school and she has a vision board for a reunion of your senior year and we can't get rid of her and helppppppppppppp

But it was Noah's message that had rattled around in her mind on the thirty minute drive to the bar.

Looking forward to being your King.

"I came as soon as I could." Prim glanced around the bar and dining area. "Where is she?"

"She's in the bathroom. Get in the kitchen."

"How's Ray?" Magnolia asked, squeezing the grey water from a mop, as they entered the kitchen.

"Wheelchair bound but looking really good."

"And his son?" Aunt Aggie grinned like the Cheshire cat. "He's looking really good too?"

"He's ..." Prim huffed. "He was there. Tonight. And very keen to take Ray's role for the Wassailing. Which can't happen."

Another flutter bounced around in her stomach.

She stomped down on that flutter. And stomped on it again.

"He can't be. End of story."

Aggie snorted. "Why not?"

"He's a normie. Better if it's one of us."

"Better why?" Magnolia grinned, clearly throwing reason

down the drain, like the mop water she was emptying, and enjoying Prim's distress.

"He's irritatingly cheerful." *And beautifully inked*, she added as an afterthought. "He knows nothing about who we really are and we're just saying it's okay for a normie to have a star-ring role in a ritual with guests including werewolves from Nebraska and vampires from Europe?"

"Well, it's not like you'll let the vamps feed on him, is it?" Geri shrugged, with a smirk.

Great, now Prim was thinking about biting Noah. Or at least, nibbling around his ear. And his neck where he had a small butterfly tattoo.

Prim latched onto the first thing that came to her mind not related to nibbling. "I sorted out insurance stuff as well."

"Wow," Geri deadpanned. "Look at you flirt. Sharing insur-ance details."

"I was not flirting. I meant with Ray. I don't like him. Noah, that is. I don't date normies. Ever. At all."

"What, like, you've dated a non-magical person ever?" Geri asked, incredulous. "Not even at college?"

Fine for her to ask. Geri dated everyone and anyone. She specialized in fertility magic. Walking, breathing and eating were practically flirting for her. She oozed sexuality in every-thing she did.

"I mean, not ever again. There were a few. Certainly not high school."

Geri strolled around the kitchen, hips swaying, a finger pressed to her mouth in thought. "But weren't you going to go to prom with Noah? Didn't he stand you up that night?"

Prim swallowed hard. Acid stung the back of her throat.

"Wait a crystal ball picking minute." Magnolia set down the mop bucket and came over to pat her arm. "He did, too. I'm sorry."

It was all Prim could do not to raze their family's century old micro-brewery and bar to the ground. A prom date prank should not still cut deep. It was on her that she hadn't gotten over how Noah had left her a note, asking her to prom, asking her to keep it secret until that night and they'd walk in together for a big reveal.

She'd waited an hour and then gave up on him, and went to the prom to find him arm in arm with Monica, being crowned stupid Homecoming royalty.

Geri tutted. "Woah, your aura right now looks like a volcano."

If only she could command fire magic ...

"I'm over it. Him." Magnolia and Geri exchanged a look. "I am!" One of the indoor creeping vines broke its glass jar, rustling and reaching for her. Outside, a tree thrashed against the back window.

Prim sighed, slumping to a stool. "It was twenty years ago. It's all over and done. And I'll clean up the plant."

Lack of sleep must be behind her lack of control. Having a *pothos* shatter its glass home and a tree do that without a spell recited ... Let alone how she'd made the tree at Ray's house shake and sway, and the rose bush straining for her, like a weapon with its thorned branches.

Prim shook her head, clearing her mind. The sooner she got to bed, the better.

Just then, a shrill nasal voice piped up through the serving hatch. "Hey, hi. I'm Monica and I was just talking to one of her sisters."

Geri suddenly clicked her fingers. "Show time, Primrose."

Prim straightened. Time to face her nemesis.

Surely people changed over time.

But Prim knew she hadn't. She'd only grown fully into who she was in high school.

And as she pushed through the kitchen door and took in Monica at the bar speaking to Sam, their new bartender, she knew Monica hadn't changed either.

Monica's nose screwed up as she took in our décor choices. The Moone family joked Witches Brew was Addams Family Lite, if Gomez Addams had had a liquor license.

Monica was dressed in a lemon yellow designer pant suit, with ample cleavage visible through the cut of the lapels. A pendant hung right at the top of her cleavage, drawing attention to her breasts. Prim wasn't sure if she was wearing a top, or a bra. Monica's tits were spectacular, Prim grudgingly conceded, with no flicker of attraction. Not even a remote flutter or flicker of anything.

Nor was there a flutter of disgust, anger or even pity.

A good sign. Maybe Prim was finally moving on from high school grudges.

"Oh my god, Primmy! Look at you! Still got that emo aesthetic after all these years!"

Nope, grudges are on. "It's P-Prim," she stammered out. Somehow, after twenty years, Monica still managed to wrap a sneer around the 'ee' sound in Primmy.

Monica ignored her, placing a huge collage on the bar. 'High School Reunion' was in bold at the top.

Prim realized too late this was the vision board Geri had warned her about. Color swatches, sequins, and diagrams covered the surface from edge to edge.

"Can you believe it's been twenty years, Primmy?" Monica let out a peel of tinkling laughter.

Acid rose in the back of Prim's throat again and she swallowed hard.

Geri raised an eyebrow behind Monica, tilting her head. Everything about Geri's gesture warmed Prim's cold heart: *'want me to take her out?'*

Prim shook her head infinitesimally and Geri shrugged.

"So, I heard you were on the committee for the pagan conference—"

"CovenFest. It's a festival for witches and witch adjacent people. Pagan and Wiccan followers are welcome, but they are different to witches."

Monica sniffed. "Whatever. CovenFest. Well, it's also the perfect occasion what with Octoberfest on and Halloween to host our twentieth high school reunion." She tapped the document with her perfect chili red-painted fingernail. "And you're going to help me."

"I'm ... what now?" Prim spluttered.

Monica frowned, folding her arms. "Your aunt said you couldn't wait to get started with preparations. That you were looking forward to it?"

"Aggie said that?" Prim turned to where her sisters were hovering at the bar, listening to every word. "Where is my aunt?"

Prim scanned the room. *Damn you, Aunt Aggie, you turncoat.*

"Noah's going to be there, too," Monica gushed. "It was lovely catching up with him today and hearing his news. Especially about his new job."

"What?" Prim asked sharply, her head whipping back to face Monica.

"At the grocery store you mean."

Monica bristled. "Well, yes—"

"He showed me his latest tattoo." Monica's eyes widened. "When I saw him." What the hell was she doing?

And what job?

Monica narrowed her eyes. "He was looking forward to the Homecoming King and Queen, reunited again at the reunion. He's going to be on my table, naturally."

Prim silently sat on the nearest bar stools, letting her conference folder land on the bar with a thump.

"Why don't you tell me more about your vision for the reunion?" Prim forced out.

Resigning herself to her fate, Prim sat mute as Monica described in great detail of how the Cascade High's Class of 2004 reunion would fit right in with the Monster Mash Ball on Halloween with the most powerful witches, warlocks and magic users from across the world.

After Monica left, Prim glanced through the folder she'd been given with color palettes, menus and task lists.

She was now of the firm opinion only doom came in threes.

CHAPTER

THREE

W atching Noah come out of the back of his farmhouse and approach them through the crowd of European witches and warlocks, a group of werewolves from Nebraska while being watched by five vampires under parasols and umbrellas under the shade of a fir tree.

It was like watching an innocent lamb walk through predators.

Or, rather, a black sheep trot along blissfully unaware he was the odd one out.

If a sheep was wearing a brass circlet with deer antlers fixed to the metal and a billowing white shirt not unlike Mr Darcy about to stride across the moors of Pemberley, and tight black pants.

Noah had swept up his long hair with a hair tie and rolled up his sleeves, despite the chill of the early evening.

Prim pressed a hand to her stomach. So many damn flutterings.

"I heard he's a nurse," Geri whispered in Prim's ear. "But with those tatts, he could be a biker. Mechanic."

"Artisan baker?" Magnolia offered, amused. "Anyone has tattoos these days."

"He is a nurse," Aunt Aggie piped up, depositing the wooden bowl they would use to sip the first cider press of the season onto a table they'd covered in a tablecloth. "Specializes in kids with chronic illness."

The Moone women collectively swooned.

But not Prim, who straightened her back even straighter. "Do you know about a new job he's got?"

Aggie waved her hand. "Yep, got offered a job with Confluence Health in Wanatchee in pediatrics. Starts after Halloween or soon after, I believe Ray said."

Noah excused himself past two fire mages and headed towards them.

"Stop staring, you idiots." Prim whacked their arms and gathered them close. "Surely there is someone else here for CovenFest who could act as the King of the orchard."

Prim knew this was in vain but she thought it worth a shot.

"It's just a show tonight," Aggie said. "We aren't really aren't cleansing the orchard of evil spirits. We're showing our magical counterparts the rituals that are important to us in the apple capital of the world."

"Apples are a mystical and ancient fruit. The ritual joins the grower with the brewer and ensures a good harvest in summer." Magnolia smiled. "As brewers we cannot not do the ritual. I'm looking forward to this."

Geri frowned. "Sometimes I feel like our education as witches was very ..."

Prim scowled. "Mediocre? Back water?"

Magnolia snorted.

Geri smirked. "I was going to say niche, but your descriptions work, too. Did you see the crystal ball message from Aunt Aspidistra that The Dusty Tome has a first edition Grimm Brothers' fairytales on display for CovenFest?"

Prim had missed any messages from her older aunt. "Hence the extra security costs for the conference," Prim murmured, and then nodded in welcome to one of the auditors who'd shown up for the Wassailing.

"Aspy said she was keen to view it." Aggie rubbed her hands. "She's booked an extra long session for us to visit as a family. She says it's the Moone family long ago in Germany who were the inspiration behind Red Riding Hood."

Prim, Magnolia and Geri all frowned at Aggie. "She only says that at Christmas when she's drunk," Magnolia said.

"She does get carried away when eggnog is involved." Aggie shrugged. "Anyhoo, Prim, she'll send you a message to confirm the booking."

"Hello, my dear girls!"

Prim jumped, but it wasn't Noah. He was shaking hands with a warlock from Prague.

Instead, it was their Uncle Vinnie, who they irregularly saw, and was looking dapper in a three piece cream suit. With chunky gold rings, balding hairline, and mutton chops on his cheeks, Vinnie was the spitting image of Danny Devito, if Mr Devito was a warlock who loved to collect shiny gold rings.

Prim and her sisters all gave Uncle Vinnie big hugs.

"Can I smoke a cigar, Prim? Or is that going to upset the spirits tonight?"

"No, that's fine, Uncle Vinnie. But maybe stay away downwind of the guests."

"Your mother and father would be so proud, look at the three of you." Vinnie beamed. "The world of magic users are gathered to admire you all."

But not in my orchard, Prim thought with a pang.

As the oldest tree was in her neighbor's back yard.

But Vinnie was right. They were on display and had a job to do. This was their chance to shine in front of the movers and shakers of their community.

Prim smoothed the front of her dress to find Noah now in front of her, looking her up and down, eyes wide.

"You're in white."

"Yes, that's the custom."

Their mother had always insisted that a maiden of Wassailing could never be dressed in black. Every year when Prim had asked why, she'd reply: *because it's pure* which Prim had found very odd. When Prim had turned eighteen, her mother had given her a different answer: *Because it's all of the colors all at once.*

When Prim had challenged this new answer, her mother had curtly replied: *Black is no color. Black is nothing.*

Black wasn't nothing. Black was simply the state of things without light. Some found comfort in that, like a weighted blanket. Like Prim.

Noah's words brought her out of her memories. "But you *never* wear white."

"Well, I do for this every year."

"You do?"

"You'd know that if you'd come."

"I always had something to do with basketball, or training, or two years in a row I was working at that café on Front Street. It was always Pops's thing anyway. And yours."

"So, is Ray going to k—who's this inked glass of water?" Aggie asked with a wink. As if she didn't know who Noah was.

Aggie had been about to say kiss. And Prim couldn't think about that just now.

"You know this is Ray's son. Noah."

"What? The skinny kid next door?"

Noah laughed and Aggie held out her hand which he took in both of his. "Oh, you're a handsome strong man now. Look at your arms, so many patterns."

Noah looked amused than insulted, thank goodness. "Um, thank you."

"No colored tattoos?" Aggie asked, ogling his forearms and up to his biceps.

"No." Noah flicked his eyes to mine. "I prefer black."

Prim's heart pitter-pattered and she scowled. This was no behavior for a thirty-seven-year-old woman who didn't believe in pitter-pattering anything.

She smoothed the bodice of the maiden's gown and adjusted the green wreath she'd made for a crown. "We should get this started." *And over and done with.*

Geri had caught the eye of a warlock from Belgium and sauntered in his direction while Magnolia banged on a brass gong, a souvenir her late parents had bought on a tour in South-east Asia years ago. Aggie settled in her camping chair and played a solo number on her bongos.

They well and truly had the attention of the crowd now.

Noah leaned into her. "What happens first?"

"Ray didn't tell you?" Prim's heartbeat picked up. Should she have texted him? Popped by? He might be horrified at what—

"Don't worry, he told me a little." Noah shrugged like it wasn't a big deal. "But not a blow-by-blow description of what goes down at your Wassailing."

"Okay, well, Aggie will do a speech and then we'll drink from this." She picked up a centuries old wooden cup carved with apples and birds around the rim. "Tradition is we drink the first cider press from this cup. It's been in our family since … well, just since. Aggie says it's very old and we have been its keepers for centuries. Brought it out from Germany to England

27

and then the Americas. Kept it safe and we perform this ritual every year in the lead up to Halloween."

"Why do I need to wear this crown of antlers?"

"You're the king of the orchard. Or nature. This is a fertility ritual." Noah blinked and Prim felt her cheeks flush. "For a bountiful harvest in late spring and summer."

He nodded slowly. "And you're the Queen." His voice had dropped, low and deep.

"Queen of the Orchard and Queen of the Damned," Prim quipped and immediately felt foolish.

Noah nodded, but not with amusement. Then he sighed. "Monica was a bitch in high school."

Prim reeled as Aggie began her welcome speech with a joke about three warlocks walking into a micro-brewery run by witches.

She couldn't hold back her incredulity. "Then why on earth did you go to prom with *her*?"

Noah stilled, frowning slightly. "What—"

"And you two seem cozy after your grocery store catch up."

Noah frowned deeper as the crowd laughed, thankfully, at her joke and then she broke out into a bongo solo to get every-one's attention. *Not now, Aggie.* "And now! Time for the King and Queen to climb the tree and drink the first press of the season!"

Noah held out a hand. "Ready to climb the tree, my Queen?"

Another flutter, smaller this time.

A chill wind blew through the trees. It was always like this, but colder. The last hiss of the spirits in the orchard looking for a way to cling to the boughs and crawl inside the trees and take up residence, causing rot and death.

Prim could feel the earth calling to her; the energy in the orchard, even with the trees barren and bare, was strong. Seeds and roots dormant and protected in the soil hummed, ready for spring. Even though this was just a demonstration, not the true ritual itself, she could feel the orchard responding to her.

"Yes," she breathed.

Noah climbed up to sit on a thick bough in the center of the tree and Prim followed, bracing her feet on two lower branches to face the crowd.

She began an incantation about the wind to shake the boughs, for the sun to warm the earth and invigorate the trees with new growth and to bear fruit, for the flowers to spring forth and herald the change of the seasons to the bees.

"That's beautiful," Noah whispered. "Is that a poem?"

Prim faltered in her recitation.

"Those words you're saying are like a song."

In centuries times past, the Queen may have played an instrument and sung the incantation. But Prim preferred to whisper it to the wind, letting the air carry the powerful words through the trees and plants to banish ill spirits and guarantee the harvest.

"I think it's beautiful, too."

He was looking at her with those liquid puppy dog eyes of his again and she tore her gaze away to focus on the task.

"And now they kiss!" Aggie called out.

Had she finished the incantation? Where had she got up to?

Prim quickly said the last two lines as the crowd began to chant 'Kiss! Kiss! Kiss!'

Noah laughed. "Do we really have to?"

"Your father didn't mention the kiss in the tree?"

"He conveniently left that bit out." Prim opened her mouth but Noah cut her off. "But I will. It's okay."

He swallowed hard. Prim hated how she could feel her cheeks burning. "Ray would give me a peck on the cheek."

"Just the cheek, then?"

29

As he spoke, he moved closer, his breath coasting over her skin. Prim angled her mouth towards him on instinct.

"Is a kiss on the cheek enough for the ritual?" Noah's voice was rough, like it hurt him to speak.

They were so close now. Prim could feel the heat of him. No wonder he wasn't wearing a coat; he positively radiated warmth.

Focusing on his mouth, images of bud burst and bees and pollen and spring filled her mind. Fruit bearing on the branch. Flowers blossoming, angling up to the sun.

"Or on the lips? To ensure the ritual is done right?" Noah asked. "For, ah, fertility?"

His eyes glowed, fixed on her lips.

A pulse tightened her gut; warmth flooding her body.

The breeze felt tropical and humid, carrying on it the perfume of unseen blossoms.

Was this the magic of nature, or the headiness of the cider press?

"Lips," she murmured.

Noah deployed his dimples and sweet perfume of roses enveloped her. "Are you sure?" he asked. "We don't have to just because they are yelling."

Prim then realized she hadn't been listening to the crowd's nonsense. There was only this moment, here right now, being up a tree with a tattooed man wearing a deer antler crown who couldn't stop looking at her mouth like there wasn't anything else he wanted in this world.

"Do it," Prim murmured.

Noah's eyes flared and for a full second, he didn't move.

Then, his hand cupped her jaw and he leaned in, pressing his plump lips against hers.

This was *not* like his father's chaste pecks on the cheek.

Noah's kiss was tentative and gentle but also hungry, like

there was an urgency in how he pressed his mouth harder against hers, his hand searching for her waist as the wind whipped around them more and more and more ...

Before Prim knew what she was doing, she moaned, and Noah smiled against her lips. She flicked her tongue against his bottom lip and he opened his mouth for her, eager. The slide of his tongue against hers was tender and lewd at the same time. She was drunk on this, Prim thought, her head lolling to the side to angle her mouth against his, to kiss him deeper, to remember how he tasted long after this evening.

He shouldn't kiss so well. He shouldn't look this good, smell so good.

Noah had broken her heart over twenty years ago on the night of the prom.

Prim knew this was just a reenactment of a Yule ritual. Her witchy colleagues were in the audience, for goddess's sake. But she let herself be swept up in Noah's caress, and her heart soared on the rising wind, now warm and fragrant, shaking the last of the autumn leaves clinging to the boughs, leaving them bare for the winter to come.

CHAPTER
FOUR

I t had been two days since Wassailing, and that kiss, and her aunt Aspidistra was about to arrive, and Prim had a pack of werewolves unhappy they were camping in the same campground as a pack of bear shifters, and they wanted it sorted, pronto.

Fun times organizing CovenFest with merely days left before the event began.

Both nights had been sleepless, waking up from dreams where Dream Noah had done a lot more than just kiss her. Sometimes they'd been up the tree. In other dreams, for Prim had had several dreams starring her neighbor, they'd been in her bed, or a bed, and in one, a meadow of wildflowers.

Avoiding Real Life Noah since their kiss in the orchard had been relatively easy with the last minute chaos of a conference to sort out, visiting venues, overseeing the delivery of the Grimm Brother's fairytale collection and the creation of the protection wards to ensure its safety.

Until now.

Noah walked into Witches Brew during their dinner rush, holding a hand-picked bunch of red roses.

The flutters had not gone away. If anything, they'd multiplied.

"These are for you. Found them today in bloom by the porch. Extraordinary. I'd pruned that rose back while Pops was in hospital weeks ago and today it had flowers all over it."

The red roses gave her pause from the jug of cider she was pouring and her fluttering stomach. How could roses be in bloom so late in October? This wasn't right. The hint of the first winter storm was in the air. They'd had a frost five days ago, too.

"They're lovely," she managed, taking the flowers from him.

"Thought of you when I saw them."

Her heart skittered as she looked up, catching his smile.

"You haven't replied to my texts," he said, watching her put the roses in an empty water jug on the bar.

"I've been busy."

Noah smirked. "So busy you don't have time to talk about the kiss at Wassailing?"

Prim misjudged a cider she was pouring and it sloshed over the bar. She swore and wiped up the drink.

"Can I buy you a drink sometime?"

Prim froze.

"Is that a dumb idea?" Noah glanced around at the diners and drinkers all enjoying Octoberfest in full swing at Witches Brew. "You run a bar and I just asked you to have a drink with me."

"Do you mean like a date?"

Noah swallowed hard. "If you'd like. Or not. That's up to you if you want it to be a date. Happy with what you decide."

He sucked on his lips, a nervous gesture, and waited her out.

Oh, how she'd thought about those lips since Wassailing.

Geri sauntered past them, humming the familiar taunt from childhood. Earlier, both Magnolia and Geri had sung the song at full volume when Prim had arrived for her shift.

Noah and Prim, sitting in a tree, K I S S I N G...

"Y-you want to go on a date." She cleared her throat. "With me."

"I do." His voice was huskier. "Very much. If you want to."

He smiled again, holding her gaze. His sparkly eyes had her in his orbit, pulling her in, like he had gravity. Like he was a planet and she was a speck of space dust.

"Okay." She cleared her throat. "Yes."

They agreed to meet at Witches Brew after closing. Prim couldn't help but think this was a late time to meet for a date. She had so many final details to check for CovenFest but ... but his offer was too tempting. Irresistible.

What speck of space dust could resist gravity?

What harm could come from an hour or two with Noah?

What harm indeed.

Hours later, just before close, with her legs aching and back cramping, Prim took the rubbish outside to the dumpster, and saw them.

Noah and Monica in the alley beside Witches Brew.

The street band playing was loud enough that they didn't notice her hefting rubbish bags into the bin.

Monica was laughing at something Noah said – a fake laugh that even Prim could tell from her position. She watched Monica pull Noah down for a wet kiss on his lips.

Noah's hands flew to her hips.

It was prom night all over again. The note asking her to be

his prom partner, the no-show on the night, and then arriving late by herself to see him with his arm around Monica on stage crowned the King and Queen of Prom, and giving her a kiss to the cheer of the crowd.

Acid burned a hole in her gut. She stormed back inside Witches Brew, and threw the bolts across the back door before turning off the lights and then setting the alarm. And in the gloom the red rose bouquet Noah had given her seemed to glow on the bar like a beating heart. She gravitated towards the flowers, swiping her cheeks in irritation to catch the tears that fell.

She really wanted to throw them away but instead Prim pushed them aside and then fled for the stairs to Aunt Aggie's apartment above Witches Brew, intent on crashing on her couch to avoid Noah at the orchard, when her phone beeped in her pocket

> Noah: Sorry about this. Monica needed some help to get home. I'll be an hour tops

Some help. She snorted. *What, mouth to mouth?*

Storm shutters went up around her heart as she typed six words back.

> Prim: I bet she did. don't bother.

"A HEX like this needs time to steep," Prim announced to Dougie. "Much like a cursed tea, I guess. Or even a stew. Perhaps I should get a slow cooker just for making potions designed to hex others."

The potion needed to steep at least overnight, according to

the grimoire. The spell she'd found at two AM in a grimoire Aggie owned was very similar to her own she planned to demonstrate at CovenFest at her symposium. She could even present the results of this potion as a bonus for her speech.

She couldn't sleep. Couldn't get his betrayal out of her head.

So she started to work on the hex.

Making this potion for Noah was ... experimenting, really. If a normie walked in now and saw her boiling a beaker over a gas flame and adding ingredients with an eye dropper, they'd assume it was science. Maybe? Sort of? It almost was. Practically an academic exercise for a magic user. She could turn this into a journal article and discuss her findings at a future CovenFest at another symposium.

Or else, this was just spite. Petty revenge.

"Which is absolutely is not," Prim ground out to no one in particular.

Her rationalization of her potion making was interrupted by Dougie cawing and ruffling his feathers.

"Do you have something to say, Dougie?"

He narrowed his eyes for a split second. He hated being called Dougie. His full demon name was Duggonamelarcus, an unflattering Latin name for a demon of the forest who could see the imps and goblins that crept into orchards to cause mischief. The perfect familiar for a green witch who managed an apple orchard. But Prim had settled on the nickname Dougie when he'd flown into her life when she'd turned twenty-one.

She was grateful she'd brought him to Witches Brew the day before. He delighted customers by singing in the rafters and turning pages of a spell book, looking all like he was about to cast magic. The book was something Prim found online secondhand from a movie props store and was entirely harmless.

"This isn't for the young witch, is it?" he rumbled.

Oh, Miri. Prim had entirely forgotten her desperate request.

She cleared her throat. "If this is effective, I'll brew her one in a similar fashion."

Dougie made the gargling, cackling sound again. Prim had always assumed it was his way of saying he disapproved.

"The spell is calling for something 'out of place and from the heart'. Whatever could that be?"

All this work on this hex could be for nothing. She'd skipped over that vague ingredient in the early hours of morning.

But Noah's roses caught her eye.

Out of season, from the heart.

She plucked several of the dark red petals, embarrassed how she'd cried over the bouquet the night before.

"Are you *sure* he is as bad as you think?" Dougie asked.

Prim held the rose petals above the beaker when a message pinged on her phone.

> Aunt Aspidistra: Prim, I despise these modern instruments to send messages. I am confirming we shall read the Grimm Brothers first edition with the family. It's a private viewing to read the original Princess and the Frog Prince fairytale. An excellent exemplar of a hex and how it's broken. Aspidistra.

Her aunt always wrote texts like she was sending a missive on parchment. No "love and kisses" either.

"Why can't she just call it a phone?" Prim muttered.

But her aunt's message gave her an idea. They weren't going to read the first record printing of Red Riding Hood.

Aspidistra wanted the family to read about the frog prince who had to convince a princess to kiss him to break the curse.

Prim smiled, letting the petals fall into the potion. They dissolved with a satisfying hiss. A frog for a day sounded like a grand idea.

The idea of Monica, her face screwed up in horror, having to kiss a frog was also wickedly satisfying.

She sighed. But unnecessary, she thought. This was for the boy next door who broke her heart.

"Under the moon, take the form of a frog," she recited, waving one hand slowing over the potion. "When the moon sleeps, take back your true form."

She stood straight, happy with her creation. There was nothing left to do now but wait and leave the magic to do its thing.

PRIM CONTINUED to ignore Noah's texts; again, easy with Witches Brew being overrun with Octoberfest tourists for the lunch rush, and then she had yet more conference duties to sort out before the dinner rush.

Despite every table with customers and a conga line of lederhosen-clad retirees dancing their way around the tables, she looked up as Noah strode into the bar.

He was making a beeline for her.

She kicked herself for assuming that he wouldn't show up if she didn't reply to his texts.

But she wanted to curse him, right?

Right. Prim's stomach roiled slightly.

Noah gripped the bar and immediately launched into his apology.

"I'm sorry about last night. Monica needed help getting home, she was a bit messy. Too many drinks."

Prim hesitated. "You two looked very cozy together."

"Oh, no. Not at all. At least from me. I'm not interested. She was very drunk and ..." He shrugged. "You never know with rideshares. Could have been sketchy. I just wanted to make sure she got to her accommodation safe."

Prim stared the German style ceramic pint jug in her hands, ready to dry with a dish cloth. Did she believe him?

"Maybe he's actually gallant and honorable?" Dougie cackled.

Noah glanced at her crow, almost looking like he could understand Dougie.

Prim snorted at her familiar. What experience did a demon whose job was to find goblins and imps in her orchard with human dating and emotions?

"Wait, you saw us?" Noah asked.

"I saw enough."

Besides, Monica had been handsy but that kiss they'd shared had come out of nowhere.

"Nothing is happening between me and Monica." His eyes swept over her face and his softened. In pity. "Prim, I swear it. She tried to ... kiss me but she was very drunk. I caught her from falling."

She swallowed hard, placing the stein down on the bar with a thump.

"I have to go to the kitchen."

She turned on her heel, leaving the bar staff to cover drinks, as Noah called from behind. "I'll wait right here."

Dougie cackled as he skipped over the bar, past Noah and hopped through the serving hatch.

Prim picked up the beaker with her potion. She'd left it to

steeping but it hadn't been overnight, as the instructions had outlined.

"Or, we can leave it to the Fates," she whispered, as she poured some into a tasting glass and set it with two other ciders on a tasting paddle.

"Mistress," Dougie said. "Leaving anything to the Fates is fraught with danger."

"I doubt the Fates are listening to a small town witch in Leavenworth."

She didn't wait for a reply, heading back out to the bar.

Noah's face lit up as she approached with the paddle.

Her hands trembled slightly. Should she curse a normie? He had no idea what she'd done. And she'd never done anything like this before. Corporate hedge fund douche canoes were one thing to hex, but it was their systems that she'd focused on, not the humans themselves.

Prim felt a little nauseas as Noah picked up a glass, holding it up to the light.

"What's this? A different cider?"

"It's a new brew I've been working on," she murmured, her hand flying to her stomach.

It felt like something hot was writhing in her belly.

"Have you tried it yet?" he asked.

"No. It's not for me."

"Mind if I do?"

She opened her mouth to reply and he lowered the glass, waiting a beat for her answer.

Just then his mobile beeped on the bar, the screen up between them.

> Monica: Heyyy, feeling pretty good. would love to catch up again. Last night was amazing *kissing face emoji*

Prim glared at the puckered mouth on the yellow face, with the small love heart on its lips, as red as his roses in the water jug on the bar.

Noah frowned slightly, flipped over his phone, and then tipped back the glass and drank the greenish potion in one go before she could say a word.

The Fates had smiled on Prim today.

P rim had felt hollow since Noah had sculled her hex potion.

She'd asked him to leave, and he'd agreed, albeit reluctantly, walking out liked a kicked puppy.

Before the dinner shift, she'd driven back to the orchard, and then checked in on him under the pretense of delivering a casserole for Ray and to see how his recovery from his knee operation was going.

After all Noah in frog form couldn't help his father. Just because Noah was a frog didn't mean Ray had to be inconvenienced.

Ray's eyes had lit up when he'd seen her on his doorstep with the casserole, saying Noah wasn't feeling well and he was right to fend for himself.

Prim hadn't stayed longer than she had intended to keep him company because of guilt. No. She was pragmatic. It wasn't Ray's fault his grandson was a liar who seemed to have devoted his adult life to toying with Prim's affection.

Why her stomach kept churning at the thought of Noah as

a frog mystified her. Probably CovenFest anxiety. With a big dollop of Monica and reunion-induced irritation. Must be.

It was as if the thought of Monica had manifested her in Witches Brew. As oompah music cheerily blared through their speakers, Monica walked up to the bar, looking all the while like the cat who'd got the cream.

Prim berated herself in her mind for not forcing Geri or Magnolia to look after the bar. She had the facial expressions that belonged in the kitchen, not in front of customers. Or Monica.

Her high school nemesis sat down on a stool and smiled her way, and then ordered a drink from one of the wait staff.

Prim busied herself cleaning tables and topping up water glasses until she could finally not ignore Monica any longer.

"Noah was very nice getting me home safely."

No hello. No greeting. Her timing after her interaction with Noah was curious.

Prim picked up a wet pint glass and wiped it hard, making the dish cloth squeak.

"He kisses really well, too." Monica adding, smirking.

"You woke up alone, Mon. And you were wasted."

And here she was, taking Noah's word for it.

"How much had you had to drink last night?"

Monica shrugged. "A little." She picked lint off her jacket. "Noah was the perfect gentlemen."

"Why are you here?"

Monica strummed her fingernails on the bar, as if deliberating her answer. "Monster Mash Ball. Have you gone over the color schemes? I need a final decision."

Prim looked Monica in the eye and Monica looked away.

Something wasn't right.

Monica had finished her cider, leaving dregs at the bottom of her glass.

Prim picked it up. "One moment."

She turned on her heel and went to the kitchen, with Dougie after her.

Prim swirled the dregs in Monica's glass. Just like tea leaves, if you are a brewer.

"Dougie, I need your demon sight."

"There's always a price," he chirped, ruffling his feathers. "And it requires blood."

Prim inhaled a deep breath. "Apple cake for dessert." *And her dagger she used to open letters should be sharp enough.*

Dougie chuffed. "And something shiny. Gold."

He eventually agreed to a gold charm Prim had kept since she was a child. Dougie didn't need to know it had come out of a gumball machine.

She cut her palm, letting three drops of blood fall into Monica's glass and then she swirled it, letting the rich red mix with the cloudy amber cider dregs.

"Show me what I saw. Show me the kiss."

Prim braced herself as Dougie's familiar power coursed through her veins. Staring at the bloody mess in the glass, images flooded her mind.

Noah and Monica in the alley.

"Let me get you into your Uber. You shouldn't go home alone," Noah muttered, catching her arm. "Where are you staying?"

Monica giggled. "A Christmas tree farm called Pining for You. Outside of town."

That was at least a thirty-minute drive from Leavenworth and near her orchard.

Noah hesitated, taking a half-step towards Witches Brew but Monica stumbled, and he caught her.

That's when she'd seen them. Prim had thought that was a hug. Lovers laughing together.

"You're so strong, Noah. So tall." Monica hiccupped, and looked like she was about to throw up, and then mashed her face to his.

The vision wavered. Prim had gone back inside at that point and then it came back into focus.

Noah gently pushing Monica away; his face a mix of pity and mild disgust. Not longing. Not lust.

He sighed, and ordered an Uber, and kept Monica upright as they waited. It arrived in a couple of minutes, the whole time he kept Monica at arm's length. He helped her into the back seat, and then got into the passenger seat up front and stared at Witch's Brew, resigned and sad, as the rideshare whisked them away.

Prim pushed the dirty glass away and rubbed her uncut hand down her face. That hadn't been a man who had had a sensuous kiss. Or wanted one. Monica had been the one doing the touching and kissing, and hadn't been welcome.

Noah had been the one gently helping her, even as Monica had tried to take advantage of him.

Prim had a horrible epiphany. "Oh goddess, Noah might actually be gallant. Honorable."

Dougie made a rumbling noise at the back of his throat as Magnolia walked past.

"I've always thought Noah was nice," Magnolia piped up, clearing away the glasses. "Like one of the decent ones. A pity he's a normie. And that prom thing was always odd for him I thought."

Prim let her hands drop. "Why is it a pity he's a normie? And he did prank me for prom night."

Magnolia shrugged. "True about prom. Sorry. And I meant it's so much easier for a witch to date her own kind."

"But you dated normies before."

"Actually, no."

Prim startled. "What?"

Magnolia laughed. "It's true. I've only dated warlocks."

"But you've said before of local guys who were good looking and you even took Lenny Sidler to the prom. He's a normie."

Magnolia shuddered. "I never dated Lenny. I just wanted to turn up with someone to the prom. And I honestly thought you knew that I hadn't dated non-magical people."

Prim blustered and spluttered, and then groaned. "My whole world is collapsing in on itself."

"What's the shock? You've dated normies before. You said so."

"I know!"

Magnolia sighed. "You're not exactly an open book on things like dating and relationships, Prim."

That made her pause for thought. Magnolia took a tray of glasses to the dishwasher. Prim stacked several more glasses on another tray and followed her.

"I acknowledge I am very private about my dating life."

"Prim, you are beyond private. You're more like a bank vault." Magnolia's eyes darted to hers. "When you dated normies, did you tell them you were a witch?"

"No way."

Prim's hand froze in midair above the dishwasher rack. A dribble of cider dripped down on the stacked glasses.

She'd broached the subject of Wiccan and pagan beliefs with a boyfriend and a girlfriend over the years as a gateway into revealing she was a witch. One had scoffed, citing it was all load of horseshit. Her ex-girlfriend hadn't blinked an eye when she'd raised it, but then again, Prim had eventually broken up with her when she realized nothing about her seemed to interest her ex much.

Except getting laid.

And Prim had been so caught up in her witchcraft, honing

her skills as a green witch that it had suited her needs to keep her around for sex.

Wow, her past relationships had been underwhelming. Nor was Prim the model girlfriend either.

Prim lowered the glass and stood back, clutching the kitchen bench behind her.

"Are you okay?" Magnolia asked, making quick work of placing the rest of the glasses into the dishwasher.

"I'm having too many epiphanies this evening."

Magnolia, who'd lost her powers about ten months ago after a horrible car accident, seemed to be drawing out insights about Prim that no one ever had, witchy or otherwise.

"Am I emotionally stunted?" Prim asked suddenly.

Magnolia laughed but her face fell along with her laughter at the sight of Prim's face. "Oh, Prim, why did you even ask that?"

"Because I've never had a true connection with someone, man or woman, who I wanted to know I was a witch. That I wanted to share this part of me with."

"That's a pretty major part," Magnolia said slowly.

"Yeah, like, most of me."

"Hey, I can't talk. Took me ages to have the courage to leave my abusive relationship."

Magnolia bumped her shoulder against hers and Prim flung her arms around her sister. "You were amazing how you left him. I'll always be in awe of that."

None of their alarms had triggered since Magnolia had left her ex in the middle of the night from their Seattle apartment, fleeing with what she could. It was a cruel thing that she'd been T-boned in a hit and run accident that night on her way to her sisters for refuge and a new life, which had left her without powers and no explanation as to why.

I released Magnolia, and straightened my corset, ignoring

the indulgent look my sister was giving me. "I'm keen to try the German spells I found to see if your powers can be restored. I think they have merit as a solution."

"I'd love that."

"I've missed casting spells with you." Magnolia's abusive ex had kept her from her aunts and her sisters, controlling her communication and social outings. And then losing her powers was also felt by Prim and Geri. The coven had been broken. "I just miss you."

"Well, I'm here now." Magnolia smiled, cracking her knuckles. "And at least I can read old German. Who'd have thunk that my liberal arts degree from WSU in European languages would be such an asset right now?"

Prim huffed, her lips curling. Magnolia had a knack of making her smile when everything felt dark and gloomy.

Her mind strayed back to Monica's kiss with Noah. It hadn't been wanted or reciprocated.

It certainly didn't look like anything that she'd experienced with Noah in the apple tree for the Wassailing.

Prim had the grim feeling the Fates weren't smiling on her at all.

CHAPTER

SIX

L aws of physics didn't apply to the storeroom in Witches Brew.

It had been created by Prim's great-grandmother who, as the legend goes, was fed up with not having enough space for winter vegetables, pickles and bottled cider, as well as potion ingredients, spare cauldrons and brooms.

Rumor was that she also used to sneak into her storeroom for five minutes' peace from her children for a cigarette.

Prim, her sisters and Aggie still used it for the same reason, but over the decades the storeroom changed dimensions and functions depending on the intent of the person entering the space. Some days it was a boardroom with a long timber table. Other days a library when Prim needed to research, or simply just curl up with a good romance book. Sometimes it even had a window, even though the room didn't have an external wall. That they knew of, anyway.

Right now, it was an office, with a trestle table, and Prim's conference documentation and guest list, and she was expecting many CovenFest delegates to check in today.

She glanced over her To Do list for today: 25th October.

It had been two nights since Noah had been hexed. Prim had spotted him drinking hot tea, or coffee, from a mug on his front porch earlier that morning, and most importantly, he was very human, before she'd left the orchard to attend to early conference matters.

He was fine. Human. Nothing to worry about.

Noah had texted yesterday he'd been feeling sick and hoped she hadn't caught anything from him.

Oh, if only he knew she'd been the perpetrator. And there was no chance of 'catching' her hex: Prim had disposed of the rest of the potion and even threw away his tasting glass to be safe.

The hex had probably felt like a fever dream. An amphibious acid trip. Nothing more.

Coming into Witches Brew and seeing his roses fully open made her feel hollow and empty. Their beautiful old-fashioned rose perfume had every customer commenting on their beauty, both appearance and scent.

Thank the goddess, Aunt Aspidistra didn't know about her sly hexing of her neighbor. If she'd known what Prim had done …

Prim shivered. Aspidistra would *never* know what her niece had done and that was final.

CovenFest was ready, and Prim was ready to receive her aunt that evening, and the Moone women were ready for another busy day with Octoberfest at Witches Brew.

After the lunch service, she found a text from him.

> Noah: Feeling much better. Can I still buy you a drink? Maybe a coffee or tea somewhere? Or even the chocolate shop? I would love a chance to talk. Swap King's Helm stories?

How dare he use King's Helm to tempt her. She shot off a quick reply.

> Prim: I'm sorry for how I acted

Now that was a loaded message.

> Noah: you don't need to apologize

> Prim: I really do. I'm sorry.

> Noah: will you let me accept your apology over a beverage of your choice?

> Prim: maybe I can be persuaded

But could she meet him for a drink? What if she liked him? What if they hit it off? What if they kissed again?

And how could she be truly honest with him in a relationship when she couldn't tell Noah she was a green witch who had cursed him to be a frog for a day?

> Prim: just one drink

CovenFest guests began to arrive in earnest and Prim welcomed them to Leavenworth in their secret storeroom. After the last delegates – a clan of werewolves from Canada, dressed in red plaid flannels and looking like Wolverine stunt doubles – took their conference tote bags, lanyards and map to find to their designated camping site just down on the Wanatchee River near the golf course, Noah walked into the bar.

"You're here," she said lamely.

Prim winced. Clearly, he was here.

Noah grinned. "I am. Came to take you for a beverage. When you can. As a break from this, and CovenFest. My treat."

He joined Magnolia clearing plates before Prim could argue, thanking customers. He even got a tip from a group of elderly women who'd been entranced by his tattoos.

As the bar began to clear after 9:30, Noah grunted, leaning slightly on the bar.

"Are you okay?" Prim asked.

"Don't feel so good all of a sudden. Was like this two nights ago."

"Here, come sit down." Prim bit her lip, and led Noah to the secret storeroom, making her intention clear in her mind he needed a place to sit and rest.

"Wow, didn't realize you had a private room at the bar."

Now the storeroom was a small lounge, with an armchair, side table with a water pitcher and a glass, floor rug and even a fireplace crackling.

"It's, ah, newly refurbished," Prim gritted out.

Noah took a seat. "Huh, that feeling has passed now."

"Why don't you stay here while we finish up?"

"I can help—ugh." His hand clutched his stomach and Noah lowered back into the chair. "Maybe I'll rest, like you said."

Prim exited the storeroom and found Dougie at his perch with his movie prop books. Suddenly a cry and a thud came from the storeroom, followed by a very loud croak.

Prim went cold. No. *It can't—*

"You okay, Prim?" Geri called from the kitchen.

"Stay where you are!"

She held out her arm for Dougie who immediately flew over and settled on her forearm, and together they headed to the storeroom.

In the secret room, a green frog sat on a pile of Noah's clothes wearing a golden crown.

"Oh goddess, he's a frog," Prim blurted.

"I'm a frog?!" it croaked. Or, rather, Noah croaked. "You can see me, as a frog? I'm not dreaming?!"

"Oh, shit. *Shit*." This should not be. It was meant to last a day, nothing more.

Prim's palms began to sweat.

Dougie cawed. "A curse is more potent if the one who placed the curse believes they truly deserve it."

"And if the one who placed the curse has great power," Prim whispered back at her familiar.

"Or, the intention and desire of the cursor is heightened." Duggie cawed. "I warned you, mistress."

Magnolia appeared at the storeroom door. "You okay?" Her eyes widened. "Why is there a Frog Prince on what appears to be Noah's clothes on the floor?"

"I—"

"I'm a frog," Froggy Noah repeated.

Prim let Dougie take his roost on the armchair. She felt sick and hot all over. "I can explain."

Magnolia and Noah both bleated in stereo. "You can?"

"Prim," Magnolia inhaled deeply. "What's happened? Aspidistra is going to be here any moment."

What had happened? How did she even explain this? Why was Noah a frog again?

"I don't ..." Prim paused. "I do know why Noah is a frog prince. But ... I also don't know why he's a frog prince *now*."

Tonight was meant to be the night Aspidistra spoke to her about being her successor. Taking her place in the witchcraft world as an expert in hexing and cursing.

"I don't deserve to be Aspidistra's successor. Not after this."

"Is that so?" A cold voice said with a clipped English accent behind them. The sisters whirled around, and Noah hopped to Prim's shoe.

She quickly picked up Froggy Noah, shielding him from her aunt in her hands.

Aunt Aspidistra was resplendent in a black and silver velvet dress and her hair swept up in a severe bun. Her aunt cleared her throat and waited, arching a brow.

Dame Maggie Smith, eat your heart out. Aunt Aspidistra had an air of gravitas that made the Dowager of Downton Abbey look like a hippy.

"Why do you have a frog in your hands?"

Geri and Aggie had now joined the spectacle from the kitchen.

"I ... cursed someone and now he's a frog prince."

Noah blurted out a series of croaks.

"Who?" Aspidistra demanded.

Prim winced. "Noah, he lives next door. Ray's—"

"Son." Aspidistra's gaze shifted. "You kissed him at the Wassailing demonstration." A statement, not a question. Who had told her aunt Noah had stepped in as King of the orchard? Gossip among witches was an unofficial currency of their community.

"Yes, he—"

"Did the ritual upset the spirits beyond the veil?"

"Not that I am aware—no. I didn't summon any magic during Wassailing."

But the hot swirling wind when they had kissed in the tree ... Her gaze locked onto the roses in the water jug on the vase just past Aspidistra's shoulder. *And those.*

"Magic?" Froggy Noah squeaked. "You're talking like magic is real." His eyes grew comically wider. "I'm a frog and I'm questioning the existence of magic."

"He's catching on quick." Aspidistra took a step towards

Prim and Noah retreated in her hands, and she held on. "He wears a crown."

Prim nodded and Aspidistra continued without waiting for a response. "Did you read the Grimm Brothers' publication before our scheduled visit?" Her aunt asked coldly.

"No! I assure you, Aunt."

"Then what is this?" Aspidistra waved at Noah. "Party tricks? A dare? Magic is not for amusement—"

Prim couldn't hold onto her cramping guilt and her galloping fear any longer.

The dam burst.

"Aunt Aspidistra, something is dreadfully wrong and I need your help. This was a simple twenty-four-hour hex. He shouldn't be turning into a frog again. Two days had passed since he turned back and I don't know what's going on. You must make it right. Please, help me."

Prim bit her lip, as if that would prevent the tears from falling.

Aspidistra blinked rapidly, jerking her head back, as one tear, then another, and more, slide down Prim's cheeks silently. Her sisters stared in shock.

Prim *never* cried but lately it seemed her eyes were very *very* leaky.

Aspidistra flicked her cold gaze to Frog Noah and regarded him for a moment. "You went to The Dusty Tome before our family scheduled visit?"

Whatever she'd expected her aunt to say, it wasn't that.

"No, I ... what with finalizing details for CovenFest and committee meetings and Octoberfest here at Witches Brew, I've only been there to oversee the delivery of the Grimm Brothers' fairytale book. Other than that, I haven't had the chance to visit The Dusty Tome."

Aspidistra arched a brow. "You cursed him as a frog prince."

"I ... I may have been thinking of the frog prince fairytale while making the potion."

Aspidistra tsked. "What you know is the stuff of Hollywood and stories for babies at bedtime." Her aunt looked at Noah as she continued. "The Princess and the Frog Prince is said to be the Grimm Brothers' favorite fairytale. They always printed it first in their collections. And there is much we can learn from the first edition about the evil witch who cursed the hapless prince into a frog."

Aspidistra sighed, and looked back at Prim. "What remains to be seen today, Primrose, is whether you're the princess or the evil witch in this tale."

CHAPTER

SEVEN

H er aunt's words still stung. Prim had never considered herself evil, despite being very good at creating hexes.

For a green witch, her talent for hexes was unusual. But Prim loved using her knowledge of plants to make potions and brews. And loved to impress her emotionally cold, and geographically distant, aunt.

She'd never used magic for evil purposes. Her motives were to teach others a lesson. Even to serve justice.

But Noah ... her motives had been spite. She couldn't even look Dougie in the eye.

"Primrose," Noah ribbited. "Prim, we can't go yet."

His bulbous eyes appeared even more bulbous.

"What's wrong? Other than you've been turned into a frog."

Noah blinked once. Then twice.

"In my clothes, my boxer briefs." He paused, flicking out his tongue. "Are there ... any metal ..."

"Metal?" she prompted.

"Piercings?"

Prim's mouth parted and then snapped shut. "What, um, kind of piercings am I looking for?"

She bent down and lifted his boxer briefs from his pile of clothes. Good quality, cotton, brand name ones in black.

Frog Noah croaked, as if groaning. "Barbell piercings."

"Oh." She gently shook his boxer briefs but nothing fell out. "How many? Where—"

"I have a Jacob's ladder," he blurted. "Three of them."

"Ohhh." Prim put him down beside his clothes. She did a quick search but no metal piercings could be found.

"Then," Noah croaked. "You'll have to ... Can you please ... check me?"

The horror of it dawned on Prim. Noah was asking her to flip him over and inspect his froggy form for penis piercings.

Her cheeks instantly heated.

"Of course." Wait, his dream. "You said you dreamed you were a frog. Did you wake up with your piercings intact?"

"Yes. Wait, are you saying that dream was real?"

Noah's eyes bulged.

Prim winced. "I am."

Noah made a noise like a drawn out ribbit. "My piercings were fine the day after that dream."

"Good, that suggests your piercings are a part of your transformation." Noah narrowed his stare. "Not 'good'. Obviously." She cringed. "I mean they should be okay."

"But ... can you check? To be sure?"

Prim gulped. "Would you rather a veterinarian to do it?"

"No!" A fly buzzed between them and Noah's tongue darted out, catching it and then swallowed hard. "Fuck, I just ate a fly. Just ... please check."

"Okay. Of course. It's the least I can do. Check if the metal you willingly put in your body for personal adornment is still there, safe and sound."

She picked him up. "Ready?"

He moved his froggy head in what she assumed was a nod, and then quickly flipped him over.

He had three black ridges with rounded ends near where she assumed a frog's reproductive organs would be. "H-how many piercings did you say you have?"

"Three," he croaked, legs flailing.

She flipped him back over, clearing her throat. "There are three lines down there. Uh, they are like your tattoos on your green skin. I think ... the lines look like barbell piercings."

"Right. Right. Good." Noah breathed in and ribbited.

They regarded each other for a long moment. Prim's mind spun, trying to catch up on the absurdity of the situation when Noah piped up. "You're a witch."

"I am."

She waited, holding her breath. Now was the moment of truth. A normie knew her true self; apple orchardist with witchy tendencies, occasional barmaid and hexes on request.

He'd said it so matter-of-factly. But then again he was a frog. Was this shock? Would he start screaming? Yelling?

Prim let out her breath in a rush. "I'm so very sorry about this."

"I'm sure you didn't mean it. You know how to fix this, right?"

Prim felt the blood drain from her face.

"You *did* mean to turn me into a frog?" Noah croaked.

She winced, covering her face with her hands. "It wasn't meant to be like this. At all."

Outside, Aspidistra called for all of the Moone women to come.

59

"It's time for the bookshop visit," Prim mumbled. "Maybe we'll find answers in the Grimm brothers' stories."

"Maybe?" he croaked. "You don't know what to do?"

Prim swallowed hard. "We'll find out. I promise. There's a story about the princess and the frog prince in the Grimm Brother's collection and it might hold the key of how to undo this spell."

"And I'm a frog."

"With a crown," Prim noted. "It's very similar to the antler crown you wore for Wassailing."

"Just kiss me, like in the kid's story."

Woah, wait a magic wand waving minute.

It was so simple. Just, kiss the frog already.

"Okay, I guess ... Yeah."

She held out her hand for Noah to climb on. His froggy skin was damp and cool to her touch but not gross or slimy or whatever she'd been expecting.

"You might have poisonous secretions. Or produce a toxin in your skin that produces hallucinations."

Noah cocked his head slightly to the side. "We are running out of options here, Prim."

Prim nodded and slowly raised him up to eye level and they regarded each other. "Right. A kiss."

"This is not how I thought a second kiss with you would go down."

Prim blinked. "You've thought about kissing me again?"

He ribbited. "The kiss in the tree was ... compelling."

Prim cleared her throat. "Not the time, not the point. Okay. A kiss."

She puckered up her lips and gave him a quick peck, half on his lips and half on the side of his froggy face.

It wasn't as horrible as she thought it would be.

She'd had worse kisses with warlocks and witches, if she was being completely honest.

"Is the magic working?" Noah croaked.

"Do you feel ... different?"

She could see the faint and rapid beating of his little heart against his chest.

"No? I don't think anything's happening."

Prim's own heart sunk. "I'm most likely the evil witch in the story, not the princess who will rescue you. We may need to find someone else who needs to kiss you."

Noah said nothing and Prim lowered him to his clothes on the floor.

Her phone beeped with a notification and he jumped.

"Would you mind taking photos of me on your phone?" Noah asked. "I can't see and I can't move like a human body can. I think it would help to deal with whatever is happening to me."

Prim sprung into action and took several photos of Noah in his frog form, including photos of the markings she assumed were his piercings at Noah's insistence.

Aspidistra called for everyone to hurry up as Prim quickly showed Noah the photos.

"I think you're right about those markings. And the crown is weird, but definitely like that frog prince in the fairytale story." Noah shifted his front feet. "Do you think we'll find answers in a Grimm brother's story for kids?"

"They collected folklore. This is a first edition of their collection of folk tales." Prim cleared her throat, her confidence rising. "Details can be lost over the centuries, with different editors and translations. Going to the original publication was the best way to find answers." She glanced back at Noah. "Definitely. And if anyone knows Brothers Grimm and hexes, it's my aunt."

Her sisters passed Aspidistra at Witches Brew's entrance. "Hasten, girls. We must hurry."

Prim rankled at the use of 'girls'. She was thirty-seven, for crying out loud. Almost thirty-eight.

As she was about to walk past her aunt, with Noah safe in her hands, Aspidistra held up a hand making her stop.

"Primrose, I don't know what got into your head to curse the boy next door, but know I am most disappointed."

CHAPTER

EIGHT

A s the Moone family walked to The Dusty Tome up
Front Street, Noah asked for the third time the same
three questions about his present situation.

"You made a potion for me?"

And Prim muttered the same answers, this time to her
corset.

"I did."

"A hex."

"It was."

"And you're a witch." The way he said witch was swallowed up with a nervous ribbit.

"I am," she answered with a sigh. "I'm so sorry."

"And a bookshop has the answer to my current situation?"

The Moone family stopped outside The Dusty Tome. The
bookshop was lit up with a golden glow. Several witches were
inside inspecting the shelves.

"I hope so. Know!" she corrected quickly. "Know so."

Geri leaned into Prim. "Protection wards are holding up.
Great job."

"It wasn't me. Lola on the committee specialising in them."
Prim had a pang of guilt at how she'd offloaded decorating the
gym for the high school reunion onto Lola as well. Lola may
well need to cast protection wards on herself from Monica's
vision board.

"Still great even though I know you're ..." Geri looked
meaningfully at Noah peering over her neckline. "Dealing with
an amphibian issue."

Noah croaked. "Are all of your family witches as well?"

"We are, green guy." Geri winked. "Come from a long line
of witches. Originally from Germany in the Black Forest, via
England for a few centuries, and then America."

"Right. Of all the apple orchards in all of the world, she had
to live next door to mine."

Before Prim could say anything to that, the bookshop
owner, Raurí, opened the door and ushered them inside.

She scooped out Noah and placed him on a shelf at eye
level. She allowed herself to be distracted for a moment,
looking at the dark romance titles behind him. Raurí also had
the new HM Hodgson special edition hardcovers with shiny
skulls on the covers and the debut urban romance mafia
romance with fantasy elements by Sarah Richhelm.

"Of all the shelves I could have chosen to put you on, it had
to be romance."

"Shit, predator threat at ten o'clock!"

Noah jumped straight into her corset again as Sigmund the
bookshop cat with his black and white tuxedo markings
stalked along the top of the shelves.

Sigmund swished his tail. He was definitely eyeing off Frog
Noah as a potential snack.

"Okay, stay put. At least my corset is hands-free and
safe."

Noah wriggled and squeaked.

Prim held her hand to her corset for calm. "It's okay. You'll be able to see the Grimm Brothers book from there, too."

"I'm not used to being in your bra!" he hissed, and then croaked.

Suddenly Prim felt wet in her corset. "Did you just--?"

"Yes! I peed in your corset!" he croaked. "I'm a frog, Prim! With a bladder the size of a peanut and it was a bit of a shock to suddenly be in your ... your ..."

"Breasts," Prim muttered, dabbing tissues to her corset. "It's okay. Peeing is what frogs do when afraid. Peeing on me is the least of what I deserve."

"Don't say it like that," Noah muttered back. "And I'm not afraid of your breasts."

They caught each other's eyes. Noah smirked and made a noise not unlike a laugh. Prim snorted and then laughed as well.

"Primrose!" Aspidistra called from a side room.

Sigmund hissed and ran off.

Their laughter faded. *Right. Hex reversal. Right.*

"So, Aspidistra is intense," Noah murmured as Prim and her sisters scuttled past the romcom and paranormal romance sections. Both Geri and Magnolia making comments about Rauri's excellent titles and authors in stock.

Maybe once this hex botch-up and CovenFest was done and dusted, Prim could come back and raid his shelves for some spicy reads and excellent book boyfriends and girl-friends.

"Aspidistra is difficult. Hard. Cold. And absolutely the top of her game for hexes."

"So she's the most likely person on earth who could solve my frog problem, and she's also a cold, hard bitch?"

Prim burst out laughing for a full two seconds, mostly in surprise. Frog Noah appeared to be smiling. "Never, and I say, never say that out loud again. In fact, she may have heard you already with some sort of spell that keeps tabs on anyone gossiping about her."

"But she's your aunt. Aggie is an amazing, friendly woman. How can one aunt be so lovely and the other is Aspidistra."

"Some people are warm and sunshine, and others are ... not." Prim shrugged. "Like me."

"You are sunshine, Prim."

She snorted. "I am the Queen of the Damned."

"That was your nickname in high school," Frog Noah frowned, or so it appeared with his forehead. "I thought it was an insult."

Prim shrugged, causing Noah to fall against one of her breasts. "It was but I made it my own."

Noah steadied himself between each of her breasts. "I punched two guys for calling you that behind your back."

Prim took a couple of steps back away from the round table set up for viewing the Brothers Grimm Fairytales, and her family.

"You did what?" she hissed as quietly as possible.

Noah tried to raise one of his froggy shoulders like it was no big deal. "I got suspended from the basketball team for two games for my one and only moment of violence."

"I ... don't know what to say."

He held her gaze with his big froggy eyes. "You're more than a nickname. You're like an earth goddess the way you inspect the orchard, like you're greeting each of the trees. You welcome the dawn, as if giving the sun a personal invitation to the orchard. And when you dance in the rain, it's ..."

She did dance in the rain from time to time, to thank the earth for watering the trees. The fact that Noah had seen her do so was unsettling. "It's what?" Prim asked, breathless.

"It's ... not ..." Noah sighed. "Prim, your clothes cling to your every curve and I was just about to say it's sexy as fuck."

Something hot and lovely swirled in Prim's stomach. "You've seen me do all of this?"

"From time to time." Noah groaned and she berated herself for liking how the sound vibrated against her chest, and her breasts.

Keep it PG, Prim!

"My bedroom is on the first floor and I can see your back-yard and most of the orchard from there. And talking about you dancing in the rain while between your breasts is not a good idea."

"Or after inspecting your piercings?"

Noah croaked loudly, like he'd laughed out loud. It was hard to tell how frogs laughed. How could he be making jokes at a time like this?

Prim found her family turned in their direction.

Aspidistra beckoned her to them with a flick of her hand.

"Time to read the book," she whispered to her corset and slowly approached the table where a two-hundred-year-old book was displayed on a V shaped stand to support its spine.

White gloves were not an issue for witches who could summon the air to move the pages. Aunt Aspidistra waved her index finger in the air over the book as the Moone family all watched.

Noah glanced over her corset to look at the leather-bound tome. Gilt edges had long worn off, but there were traces here and there of the gold sparkling in the cracked leather

"What language is that?" he whispered.

"German. And it's two-hundred-year-old German too. My aunt is fluent as is Magnolia."

Green witch magic was no use tonight.

"The wicked sorceress turned the handsome king into a

toad, doomed to wait for a princess to free him from the spell," Aspidistra murmured, and then turned to face Prim. "Making you the wicked sorceress."

"Aunt, I didn't—" But she had. She did. "I was the one who was bullied and lied to. Not him. I'm not the evil one."

"You put a hex on him."

"Okay, yes, I did. But it was meant to last a day. Meant to scare him. Inconvenience him for twenty-four hours."

"And yet, here he is. There's more to this." Aunt Aspidistra tilted her head slightly. "There's a shadow about you. Are you sure the Wassailing didn't entice any spirits through the veil?"

"There was that hot wind that night when you kissed," Geri piped up.

Prim glared and she shrugged an apology.

Her sister was right. That swirling hot wind.

And the rose bush at Noah's house that had spontaneously bloomed.

"I admit that the spell felt very powerful. More powerful that I'd expect from a hex that lasts a day."

Aspidistra placed a velvet bag on the table and a beautiful snake slid out, tongue flicking. Her aunt's familiar.

Noah squirmed in her bra. "Do not let that thing near me. I am not a witch's pet's snack!"

"You're safe with me," Prim hummed. "But stay down."

Just as well she'd left Dougie back at Witches Brew. He didn't like her aunt's familiar either.

The snake rose up, looking Prim in the eye, tongue flicking in and out, and then slid up Aspidistra's arm and coiled around her forearm like a gleaming copper bracelet.

Aspidistra's eyes fluttered and then focused on Prim. "You were to take over my legacy as the leading expert in curses and hexes. CovenFest was meant to be your crowning glory. Your symposium was to stand among your peers and receive the recognition that's due to you for your work in hexes.

"But, you've done something that could undo everything you've worked for. I'm afraid, dear Primrose, you've managed to hex yourself, along with this man who lives beside your orchard."

"It's Noah Fitzgerald," her corset muttered but Aspidistra paid him or her corset no attention.

"Only you can break the spell."

BACK AT WITCHES BREW, Prim left Noah on the bar while she spoke with Magnolia and Geri.

"The new moon is on the first of November," Geri pointed out on the calendar in the kitchen. "Halloween will be cloaked in darkness when the veil is thinnest."

"And the new moon is about banishing things out of our life, getting rid of bad things," Magnolia added.

Prim's insides cramped up. Good goddess, she'd made this hex in the lead up to a new moon on one of the most significant nights of the witch year.

She'd managed to work into a hex a Marie Kondo style of witchy decluttering. Does your ex-boyfriend spark joy? Hell no! Do you despise the man next door? Then yeet him at Halloween on the new moon!

"And only you can fix this, Primrose."

"Of course I want to fix this. I'm not happy about this! I'm not slacking off!"

Magnolia squeezed her upper arm. "I know you're not. I meant for this hex, I believe you are both the princess and the evil sorceress. Therefore, only you can unlock your spell and save the prince. Maybe the answer isn't in books, it's with you."

Prim scoffed and took off, heading for the back door, which she let slam close before she settled on a milk crate.

A smelly alleyway seemed appropriate as a metaphor for her life right now: feeling like trash.

A rat darted out from under the Dumpster and then ducked back underneath as Magnolia came out the back door.

Her sister sat down beside Prim on another milk crate and they both stared at the waning crescent moon.

"We'll figure this out," her sister murmured.

"We haven't figured out why you lost your powers after that car accident last year on winter solstice. Why do you think we can do break this hex?"

Prim immediately regretted her bitter words and turned to her sister, chest heaving. Magnolia's lips were set in a grim line.

"I'm so sorry, Mags. I didn't—"

"You're right. We've been up against a brick wall trying to solve why I lost my powers." Magnolia's eyes burned. "So, then, do we just give up on Noah and buy him a terrarium to live out his froggy days?" Magnolia stood and stepped away. "Pet shop will be open tomorrow at nine. I'll see if they have amphibian tanks."

"No, no! There has to be a way to fix this!"

Magnolia's face softened. "That's right, there is. Prim, you are the most powerful witch who can cast curses and hexes. I believe you can do it."

Prim felt her cheeks were wet and she sniffed several times. "I don't deserve a sister like you. How do you do it?"

"Do what?"

"Be so damn positive in the face of absolute shit?"

Magnolia never complained that she was the one witch

who'd turned into a normie. She never complained she was left out of spellcasting. Yet here Prim was, spiraling into despair since her hot-headed curse.

"You're being too hard on yourself," Magnolia said softly.

Prim cried out, wiping the tears from her eyes. "Too hard? Not hard enough. I acted so inappropriately and I've ruined Noah's life."

"You could keep blaming yourself and hosting a pity party for one or you could work out how you are going to give him his human life back."

Prim nodded vigorously. "If the key to breaking the hex is that I am both the wicked sorceress and the princess, I just don't know what it means."

"We'll figure it out."

"I kissed him as a frog and nothing happened."

Magnolia nodded slowly. "Actually, I'm surprised none of us had asked if that had been explored as an option."

"The fairytale talked about slamming him against a wall and I can't do it. I won't. It will hurt him and I can't do that."

"I don't think the fairytale is literal." Magnolia squeezed Prim's arm again. "We'll figure it out."

Magnolia went back inside Witches Brew and Prim indulged herself a moment longer to herself in the alleyway, staring at the sky at the moon.

The sliver of curved silver in the sky was now a ticking clock, counting down Noah's doom.

She shuffled back inside to find her sisters in a discussion with Noah about where he could stay for the night.

Prim swore under her breath. Of course he couldn't turn up to his father's farm as a frog.

"I can call Ray and say Noah is running late tonight. We can wait here until he transforms back."

"If he does," Aggie murmured. All three sisters and Noah

stared at her and she held up her hands in an apology. "When. When he does, of course."

But their cover story wasn't necessary in the end. An hour later, Noah transformed back into human form, with Prim carrying him into the storeroom just before he did. Prim thanked the goddess and her great-grandmother for a space where he had privacy to get dressed.

"You need a minder," Prim declared as he exited the storeroom, tucking in his shirt. "Someone to stay with you, with your clothes and phone and stuff like that, when you're a frog."

"Like, what? Stay in my room? Be my shadow?"

The ramifications of her suggestion made Prim cough. "Um, yes." She nodded, straightening her back. "Yes, someone to sleep over in case of further transformations. Your frog form isn't stable for long but it's impossible to know when you might change again. Or indeed, if you do again."

"Are you offering?" he asked, his face neutral.

Prim clutched her conference binder to her chest. "I ..." She sighed. "I guess I have to. It's the least I can do."

Noah didn't say anything until they reached his farm.

Ray glowed from his recliner when they entered his house. "Oh, look at the two of you. Been out together? Get that drink? Must have been a good drink because you're here."

Ray winked with pure glee.

"Always knew you two kids would finally see the light and get together."

Prim spluttered. "Oh, we're not—"

"Pops, it's not—"

"Oh, pish posh, don't get all millennial on me." Ray waved them off. "I may be old but I can tell when two young people are into each other and you two are. So don't come at me about labels or whatever you call dating. All I'm saying is don't feel like you need to sneak around. I ain't no prude. You're more than welcome to stay, Primrose dear."

She was blushing.

Noah looked ... Prim didn't know how to describe it. His jaw ticked before he awkwardly laughed.

"Thanks, Pops." He swallowed hard, his Adam's apple bobbing. "Much appreciated."

"You're welcome."

They both trudged up the stairs to his room, Noah whispering instructions which room was his.

After closing his door, Prim pounced on the conversation. "Fake dating allows me to shadow you while we figure this out. So while this is embarrassing and highly unbelievable, we can lean into this story that we are together in order to break this hex."

"Right," Noah replied tightly. "You need something to sleep in."

"I ..." She was about to refuse but he was right. "Yes, please. If you have something."

He handed her a soft black tee shirt that came to her mid-thigh. It was more nightie than tee shirt.

"Bathroom is just down the hall."

After showering, Prim found Noah already asleep, with a row of pillows down the center of his large bed. She hesitated, watching the rise and fall of his chest as he breathed deeply.

"Don't be weird, Prim. Just share the bed," he muttered, cracking open an eye, and then rolled over.

She quickly settled on the mattress and then lay there for several moments reeling how her life had come to this.

"Good night, Primrose," Noah said gruffly, his voice rough with sleep.

CHAPTER

NINE

The next day, Aspidistra tried a hex-breaker spell that had made her famous in the eighties. But Noah remained resolutely still a frog.

CovenFest was launched, but Prim did the minimum she needed for it, immediately heading back to Witches Brew, and then Noah's farm, missing the Spiral Dance. A storm hit just as they arrived at Noah's, and with Ray they watched the rain and lightning together, until Noah felt the change – a spike of energy down his spine, he'd called it.

The morning after was grey and overcast as Prim then fronted CovenFest for her symposium, with her notes and slides on SpellNote.

And then she'd cancelled her presentation, leaving the room in an uproar. Prim had hid like a coward in the storeroom at Witches Brew all day away from gossip and the committee. Dougie and Noah kept her company, reading grimoires, old journals from ancestors and magical texts researching anything and everything about hexes.

The next day, Prim had forced herself to face conference

guests and the committee about cancelling her symposium, citing she had been unwell. She busied herself with conference administration and joined Dougie and Noah for research with her sisters after Witches Brew closed for the night. At her sisters' insistence, Prim went with them, with Noah tucked into her corset, to the markets, combing the stalls for any ingredients, potions, spells – anything that might help them unhex Noah.

After late nights with her sisters and Aunt Aggie after long days at CovenFest, Prim found herself waking up at the table in their storeroom more than in her bed.

Noah had transformed back into human form twice again and had spent time with Ray. Prim and her sisters made sure Ray was taken care of as well with his recovery and meals.

After two more failed attempts to reverse the hex and only one day until Halloween, Prim knew tomorrow night was their deadline.

With Noah in frog form much longer than human form, it felt like the hex was taking a permanent hold.

She found herself waking up at the table in the Witches Brew storeroom on the thirtieth of October with no recollection she'd fallen asleep. Drool had dried in the corner of her mouth.

Her eyes fluttered open. There were voices. Dougie was carefully turning the page of an old book with his talons.

"This author was a contemporary of the Grimm siblings. We are looking for old magic. Folklore." Dougie ruffled his feathers. "The stuff of the crone in the forest cursing a hapless noble."

"But there was no reason for why the noble in the frog prince fairytale was cursed," a croaky voice answered. "And there's no evidence it was a crone who was the 'evil sorceress' in their fairytale either. In fact, those damn Grimm brothers could have given us a lot more detail about many things."

She straightened and Dougie skipped to the side.

"Good morning, mistress," he said.

"You're working together?" Prim yawned and stretched. "I'm sorry I should be—"

Noah hopped over to her. "You've been working during the day and night. You needed rest and Dougie can turn the pages. We make a pretty good team."

Prim glanced at Dougie. If a crow could roll its eyes, that's what Dougie was doing.

The next day after CovenFest activities, they met again with Prim's sisters in the storeroom.

Geri paced with her iPad, clicking between open tabs, her eyes flicking swiftly across the screen.

"The original version of the fairytale talks about a faithful servant Heinrich, or Henry, had iron bars around his heart to stop it from breaking over his master's curse."

Noah's forearms tensed, his hands gripping the table. "Iron bars?" he rasped.

Prim's eyes flicked up to him.

"Are you okay? Are you about to turn again?"

"Hear me out, I think my piercings are like my tatts. When I transform, they become a part of Frog Me. Like the crown. At first I thought they fell out or something when I first transformed into a frog and I looked for them, and found nothing. It's only my clothes that don't transform and I have a theory it's because they aren't inside me, not like my tattoos are ink under the skin and like my piercings are inside my—" He waved frantically over his crotch. "My, um ..." He waved again, staring at her.

Prim's breathing hitched, the ramifications of how he'd spent months healing to augment his body for pleasure.

She cleared her throat. "The iron bars were holding his man servant's heart together to stop it from breaking." Prim paused. "Not his ... penis."

"Clearly, they were lovers," Geri said, entering the kitchen just as the kettle whistled. Prim and Noah sprung apart. When had they moved so close together?

"I'm surprised the Grimms didn't say they were room-mates," Geri continued, getting teacups unaware of Noah's penis revelation. "The prince does his duty and marries to continue his blood lines but his man servant is in love with him and carries out his dutiful service until he dies. The end."

"The Grimms published a queer love story as the first in their fairytale collection and are on record that their favorite tale they'd recorded was the Frog Prince," Magnolia added, getting the tea. "Just saying."

"I don't have a gay lover or a gay employee or someone in my service who is in love with me." Noah held up his hands, glancing to Prim. "Or any lover whatsoever. Just so we're clear."

Later, on the drive to Noah's house, Noah asked about Wassailing.

"So, I get it's a tradition to cleanse the goblins from the trees. But why do you host it every year at our place? I mean, you have a whole orchard but you always want the King and the Queen of the orchard in our tree."

"It's to honor the oldest tree in the district."

"But it's not."

"What? Yes, it is!"

"No, I mean that tree you always have the ritual in, it's not the oldest tree. In the thicket on the southern side of our property where the fawn lily grows, there's an older tree. Pops told me before his knee operation. Slipped my mind until now."

"An older tree?"

"Absolutely." Noah paused. "Could that have affected my hex? Using the wrong tree for the ritual?"

Prim sighed. She'd thought the same thing several times these past few days. "I've already discounted that theory. It was a reenactment but there was that hot wind, which was unusual. And the way your rose bush bloomed in the middle of autumn." Prim folded her arms. "I'm a green witch. And that was magic. I'm sure of it. No other explanation for it. Sometimes nature responds to my magic, sometimes on just feelings alone. Not often. Like I can count on one hand the number of times it's happened. Often when I was angry or frustrated."

"I kissed you that night."

"Yes, you did."

"It was a good kiss."

Prim felt her cheeks heat up. In the last week, this was the most she'd blushed, sighed and cried.

"It was."

"Do you think your magic responded, or activated, or whatever it's called, to your feelings about the kiss?"

Noah wasn't looking at her. He flicked a page, and then another, of a grimoire, looking casual.

Her nerves, however, were like a livewire.

"I ..." She had thought about the kiss a lot. "It's possible."

"And the roses flowering on the bush by our porch. That's weird, right?"

Prim nodded. "Very. It's possible that when we enacted a fertility ritual that my feelings called to magic and made the flowers bloom."

He nodded, saying nothing, as she parked in his drive, and headed inside, saying hello to Ray.

Prim left Noah to help his father to bed. He was healing well and didn't need a wheelchair anymore and was doing short walks each day.

Prim made sure she had showered and was in bed before Noah came to his room. He changed in the bathroom and slipped into his bed, and they lay there silent.

She thought he'd gone to sleep when he suddenly spoke. "You awake?"

"Just."

He rolled over to face her in the dark, his eyes glowing in what little ambient light there was in the room. "I was thinking. I should have asked you out sooner. I'm sorry I didn't. Night, Prim."

She didn't fall asleep for ages after that admission from Noah and when she woke, the line of pillows had been pushed aside his body flush with her back, and her arm wrapped around his hip, clinging to him.

G eri paced with her iPad, clicking between open
tabs, in the storeroom where grimoires and spell
books were open on a long table. A whiteboard was
set up in a corner with notes. The storeroom was being referred
to as the 'war room' this week, with research efforts intensify-
ing. Aunt Aggie and Aspidistra were consulting with CovenFest
delegates while Prim and her sisters managed the war room
and the lunch and dinner service at Witches Brew.

With one night left before Halloween, everyone's nerves
and energy levels were high and frayed. It hadn't helped when
Prim had forgotten about Alwyn and his request a few days ago
but she was pretty sure she'd faked her forgetfulness. And
thank goodness her aunts had finished Alwyn's potion. She
didn't trust herself making anything right now.

Not to mention Alwyn noticing Noah at the bar in frog
form. And how after Alwyn had left, Noah had casually asked
how Prim knew Alwyn and whether they were close. And how
rattled she'd felt when he had asked that.

Prim's thoughts came back to the task at hand as Geri

whistled for attention. "Let's go back to the original version. The fairytale talks about a faithful servant Heinrich, or Henry, had iron bars around his heart to stop it from breaking over his master's curse."

Noah's forearms tensed, his hands gripping the table. "Iron bars?"

Prim's eyes flicked up to him.

"Are you okay?" Magnolia asked. "Are you about to turn again?"

Noah glanced at each of her sisters. "Hear me out, I think my piercings are like my tatts. When I transform, they become a part of Frog Me. And I'm assuming the crown is because I was King of the Orchard, right?"

Prim sucked on her lips. Maybe? It was a good theory so far.

Her breathing hitched, the ramifications of how he'd spent months healing to augment his body for pleasure. She cleared her throat. "The iron bars were holding his man servant's heart together to stop it from breaking." Prim paused. "Not his ... penis."

"Clearly, they were lovers," Geri declared. "Was that what you were going to say, Noah?"

Prim and Noah sprung apart. When had they moved so close together?

"I, ah ..."

Geri continued, oblivious to Noah's stammering and Prim's red cheeks. "I'm surprised the Grimms didn't say they were roommates, like every other historian glossing over queer love in history. Anyway, in their tale, after the prince gets his human form back, he does his duty and marries the princess to continue his blood lines, but his man servant is in love with him and carries out his dutiful service until he dies. The end."

"The Grimms published a queer love story as the first in

their fairytale collection and are on record that their favorite tale they'd recorded was the Frog Prince," Magnolia added, getting the tea. "I think that's quite progressive for the early eighteen hundreds. Just saying."

"I don't have a gay lover or a gay employee or someone in my service who is in love with me." Noah held up his hands, glancing to Prim. "Or any lover whatsoever. Very single. Just so we're clear."

Since that discussion, sleeping in his room, and bed, had felt more intimate, more intense.

Prim was aware of his every movement, every breath, and not just if he turned back into a frog. It felt like she was now in tune with him.

And the domesticity of it all heightened this feeling. How they charged their phones side by side. Her clothes now had a drawer and hanging space in his wardrobe. Her favorite pillow on his bed. If Noah woke before her, he left a steamy hot cup of coffee on the bedside table.

Their mornings and evenings bookended CovenFest, with Prim attending workshops and keynote speeches for any clue or extra ideas of how to break the hex.

After days of dead ends and failed spells, Prim found herself clutching her fifth coffee like a lifeline after a presentation on love potions, and paused at the doorway to the secret storeroom, watching Dougie and Frog Noah.

"What if ..." Noah croaked. "What if this hex is more like Beauty and the Beast, than the Frog Prince?"

Dougie ruffled his feathers. "Beauty and the what?"

"Beast. There was that rose in the glass and petals falling, like a countdown clock. And the rose bush at my place bloomed overnight after the Wassailing. The same roses on the bar."

"Curious. And did the Beauty or the Beast cry on the roses?"

"Cry? What? No, it's in this glass case, right? One rose, not a bunch. No tears can fall on the rose." Noah hopped to a saucer where dark brown liquid had been spilled, or poured, into it. "Why do you ask about tears?"

Dougie tilted his head. "Mistress was very sad about something you did. About the prom."

"Prom?" Noah asked. "Prim was crying?"

Prim cleared her throat, and they looked to her as she entered, closing the door behind her. "How's research going?" she asked, deflecting the conversation. "How can I help?"

"We have several grimoires that look promising. Dougie has found a hex breaking spell using rose petals from Estonia," Noah said rapidly. "And putting it out there. Beauty and the Beast. Clearly, I'm the beast and you're the beauty in this tale. Who wrote it? Was it a Grimm? Both of them?"

"It was Madame d'Aulnoy," Prim picked up a saucer of dark brown liquid beside Noah and sniffed. "Is this cold coffee?"

Noah blinked quickly. "Aggie poured some for me. It's really strong."

"Have you slept?"

"Nah-uh. Been working through the night researching with my demonic buddy, Doug."

"Surprisingly, we work well together. Noah is a creative thinker, especially with coffee."

"High five, research bud."

Noah held up one of his frog feet and, to Prim's complete shock, Dougie held up a talon and bumped it against Noah's foot.

Prim couldn't help but feel a certain sense of pride, despite their dire situation.

"Well, no more coffee for now." She set the saucer of coffee aside. "Not sure what your frog heart can handle."

"So this Madame Dal—" Noah began but stumbled on the French name.

"Madame d'Aulnoy," Prim repeated. "A Frenchwoman who held salons in Paris telling stories with other writers. She wrote more than a hundred years before the Grimm Brothers."

Frog Noah smiled and Dougie tilted. "You can be impressed at my knowledge but I confess The Dusty Tome had a copy of "The Bee and the Orange Tree" by Melissa Ashley two months ago. It was a great read about Madame d'Aulnoy. I went down a rabbit hole about French salons and fairy tales."

"Why were you crying about prom?" Noah asked.

"I'd seen Monica. She raised how I'd been pranked for prom."

"What happened?"

"She'd given me a note in high school two days before prom that appeared to be written by you. And it was asking me to go to prom with you. You asked me to just nod if I wanted to go to prom next time we were at the lockers. And I did and you kinda just looked at me, but then you smiled and nodded back. And then we had to get to class, and I thought we had a secret. But prom night came and you never showed up to take me, and I turned up an hour late to see you kiss Monica as the Prom Queen."

Magnolia rapped on the storeroom door, calling for all hands on deck to help wait tables. Prim sighed, and left with Geri, and worked for hours with the busy Octoberfest crowds, noting a few delegates from CovenFest at tables for the evening.

She was spent when her family closed for the evening and she drove Dougie and Frog Noah back to Ray's house.

By the time she'd showered and brushed her teeth, it was after midnight.

Frog Noah was on the floor, sitting in his water bowl she'd set up for him to keep hydrated in frog form.

"So, you liked me in high school."

Prim almost missed the bed as she lowered herself to sit. "What do you mean?"

"You were excited about me asking you to prom." Noah croaked and attempted to shake his head. "To think after all this time, you had a crush on me in high school."

So he'd been thinking about the note and Monica and prom all evening. "That's your takeaway from earlier?"

"Not the only takeaway."

Prim's mouth twitched.

"You really thought I'd pranked you," Noah ribbited softly.

"Yeah, I did."

"Hence the hex."

He said it so matter-of-factly. Shame washed over her. "It was childish and stupid and—"

"You were hurt. And she was still holding that insecurity over you only a week ago."

"I even did a spell with Dougie, had to cut myself and use blood for Dougie to show me what really happened with you and Monica that night at Witches Brew."

Noah blinked. "And what did you see?"

"What you told me."

She hiccoughed and Noah hopped over to her, and Prim picked him up with care and laid back on the mattress, sitting him on her stomach.

"Prim, I never gave Monica a note. And that kiss on stage meant nothing," he said. "It was a polite way to congratulate her on being crowned, nothing more. Even the school staff encouraged me to kiss her for photos, which was kind of gross looking back now."

She nodded, facing the truth after so long. "Monica wrote the note. I'm sure of it."

The way Monica had made that snide comment about the prom and Noah when she had arrived in Witches Brew with her vision board. *Grrr.* Prim took several deep breaths to settle her blood pressure.

"She pranked me, and because my toxic trait is not getting over stupid things teenagers do in high school as well as not learning how to communicate effectively about something that upset me, I've turned you into a frog."

"Hey, we'll solve this."

His froggy rumbly voice was oddly comforting. "We will, Prim," Noah insisted. "There has to be a way. Just how powerful a witch are you?"

"I'm considered a leading expert in hexes and curses. You're taking my revelation of being a witch rather well."

"Oh." Noah swallowed hard. "To be honest, it kinda makes sense, given what I've seen over the years. Dancing under the full moon with your sisters, speaking to your apple trees, and your crow, which I now know you were having a two-way conversation with Dougie."

Prim huffed, making her belly bounce. Noah jumped to the side and croaked.

"I just want to reassure you, Prim, I didn't go to the prom with anyone. I didn't send you that note. And I didn't lead you on asking you out for a drink. I wanted to spend time with you. Still want to spend time with you. Liking too much how you are staying over in my room and my bed when I should be focused on how life as a frog is not a great outcome at all."

Prim's mouth parted.

"I like you," Noah continued. "I've liked you for a ... long time."

"W-what?"

"I'd always ask Pops if he knew whether you were seeing anyone and we'd always do the harvest each year helping each other but I was with Meredith and later with Jane, and you had dated men as well and the last time I saw you five years ago, you were with someone and your sisters were saying you were so in love and I thought you'd found the one at last. And I let you go. Or at least tried. Pops had said you were single again, and then to find you on our doorstep wanting to talk about Apple Day and Wassailing, I dared to hope that ... that ... you'd have a drink with me."

Noah shrugged as well as he could for a frog whose shoulder joints didn't lift like a human's. "So if you want to talk about toxic traits, add 'is attracted to women who have a dark romantasy—shadow momma vibe who might unalive them' to the list. Always had a thing for Morticia."

Prim wanted to delight in his confession, but guilt refused to let go. "I'm so sorry about this hex."

"Honestly, it's kinda hot that you were jealous of Monica and then hexed me and I don't know what that says about me but it's true and here we are."

She was speechless. Before Prim could form a coherent thought, Noah groaned, squeezing his froggy eyes shut.

"It's happening again. Now. It's like ... a spiky feeling. A tingle but with spikes. *Urgh*."

Prim scooped him off her belly and placed him beside her in his bed. "I'm right here. It's okay."

There was smoke and a cloud of color and the mattress dipped under the sudden weight of him. Prim found herself eye-to-eye with Noah, human again, and naked. He shivered and reached out to cup her jaw.

She couldn't stop a tear rolling down her cheek. "I'm so sorry."

"Can I hold you please?" he whispered. "It's so cold being a frog and I can feel your warmth from here."

Prim wriggled over, pressing her body to his, and pulled the blanket over them both.

Noah sighed. "Being in your bra keeps my blood warm." He stilled. "That came out wrong. I think?"

"Not that my boobs are anything to talk about," Prim muttered against his chest.

"I wholeheartedly disagree." Noah tutted, slowly trailing a finger down her arm. She breathed in sharply as his finger moved back and forth over her soft skin. "I could talk about your breasts for hours."

Prim whimpered as he dared to run his finger over the edge of the fabric across the swell of her breast. "Fuck. Make that days. Weeks."

Would he touch her? Would he do more, if she asked?

Could she even ask him, considering what she'd done to him?

"Can I kiss you again?"

Was she hearing things? "Why?"

"Oh, Prim." His eyes were black now, liquid. A portal to hungry, heated places. "Haven't you figured it out yet?"

His hand cupped her breast, and she was ashamed to say she leaned into his touch.

"When I said I like you, I meant it."

She gasped.

"Prim, tell me I can touch you. Kiss you."

"I don't want to take advantage of you," she breathed.

"Prim, you're not. I don't want to miss another chance to know you like this. If you want to."

She nodded, and then moaned as his fingers slipped underneath the fabric. He looked as affected as her, his hand trembling. "Am I too cold? Being a frog is leaving me cold blooded even in human form."

"I love how cool your fingers are."

"You are so warm. You radiate heat."

Her heart thudded at his words. "My magic is governed by the sun, not the moon."

His hand stilled. "Yeah? Oh, because you're actually a nature witch. Plants and stuff?"

She smiled. "A green witch."

Noah's face lit up. "That's why you're the one who runs the orchard."

She nodded. "Each generation of our family, there has been a green witch. My mother was a green witch, and her grandmother before that. I need connection to the earth, water and sun."

"You make things grow."

Prim narrowed her eyes slightly, her lips curling up. "Was that a bad joke?"

She shifted her hips slightly, pressing into his very obvious arousal. Prim could feel his piercings and it was all could do to keep her eyes focused on his face.

"Primrose Moone, did you just make a joke about my dick?"

A burst of laughter erupted from her.

Noah grinned, looking at her like she'd hung the moon. Or the sun. Both.

"I did not make a joke about your ... arousal."

"I think you did, and now that you mention it, I am very aroused right now, Prim." He inhaled sharply, his hand becoming still. "You can touch me, if you want," he added in a low voice.

She pressed her hands against his chest, her fingertips rising and falling over each of his ribs. Noah stifled a groan as she grazed a fingernail over one of his nipples.

"I used to think about you all the time in high school," he breathed as she continued her exploration over his chest. "But you never talked to me. Hardly gave me the time of day as your neighbor."

"I didn't think you were into emo girls who liked to spend more time with trees and crows than people."

"You captivated me. The wild girl always out between the apple trees, picking flowers, walking in the woods. You still captivate me, Prim."

She tore her gaze away, unable to handle how earnestly he stared at her, and found herself looking at where his dick was prodding her stomach.

"Did you want to touch me?" Noah sighed. "I don't know how long I have in human form."

"Over the years, I've thought about so many times of what I'd like to do to you. With you." Prim was panting. She'd dared to admit her thoughts to him. "But ..."

"But?" he asked.

"What if we are in the middle of something right now and then suddenly, frog prince?"

Noah let his forehead rest against Prim's. "Not awkward at all."

They both huffed a laugh despite their situation, and stayed like that for a long moment until they couldn't help themselves. Prim's hands roamed over his back and chest, tracing over the tattoos over his heart, and down his arms. Noah kissed her neck, nipping and licking, and his hips rocked into her, as if unable to help himself.

And then finally, he found her mouth with his and kissed her deep.

Her leg came up and around his waist, desperate to touch as much of him as she could, and Noah responded with a groan, gripping her ass and holding her against him.

"Fuck, I can't believe I'm here right now with you. Like this." He bit her again on her neck. "If I was a warlock, I would use every spell I knew to give me the time I needed to make you feel good. I'm guessing magic doesn't work like that?"

"No, not really," she replied softly. "Not my magic. I wish it did."

"Can I make you feel good right now? Please?" He sucked the skin on her shoulder.

Doubt and guilt seeped in her lust-addled mind. "Why?" Prim's voice was no more than a haunted breath.

"Prim." Noah held himself above her, making her look him in the eye. "I forgive you." She uttered a small cry. Her eyes stung. "I forgive you," he repeated, as a single tear escaped down her cheek.

Noah kissed her forehead. "I forgive you, Prim. Do you believe me?"

She sighed, her nails digging into his sides. Noah squirmed, his face contorting in pleasure.

"I want to."

"But?"

Prim licked her lips and shrugged, too sad to say the words. *I don't deserve this. You. To feel good.*

"Would you let me show you just how much I forgive you?"

Prim wiped a tear, and slowly nodded.

"I know I'm asking a lot of you to trust me. But I've got you, my green witch." That little possessive use of 'my' made her heart thud.

Noah sat back on his haunches between her legs. "For what little time we have, I'm going to make you feel so good. Leave you in doubt of how I feel."

THEY'D JUST SPENT over an hour together, wrapped up in each other's arms when it started.

Noah's groans instantly woke her.

"Fuck, Prim," he rasped. "It's happening. Fuck, it hurts. It's worse—"

She sat up and Noah squeezed his eyes shut, his sweet face now twisted in pain.

There was smoke and a burst of color and then beside Prim's hip was a frog wearing a crown.

They stayed like that, staring, silent.

His changes were happening more frequently now. Noah was spending more time in frog form as each day crawled to Halloween. He was meant to start as a nurse in a matter of days. He had a career and a life and she was helpless to stop this. And she'd caused it.

And she'd let him give her pleasure, pleading with her to fall between her legs and taste her. Which he had, twice, and then had come in his hand, unable to hold back his orgasm any longer, urgently whispering how perfect she was, how much he'd wanted this.

Guilt twisted Prim's insides. She shouldn't have done any of this with him. Or slept in his arms. She should be trying every waking hour to find a solution to this.

He couldn't be doomed to spend the rest of his life as a frog.

She didn't even want to think about pining for the normie next door she couldn't have. Would she keep him like she did Dougie her familiar, and he'd live out his amphibian life watching over his father and family home, unable to tell Ray what had happened and watching him grieve?

How had her silly hex come to this; ripping families apart?

She was the evil sorceress in this fairytale, Prim thought, as her tears fell.

As he placed one of his frog feet on her hand, she had the awful feeling there was no princess to save Noah from his fate.

CHAPTER

ELEVEN

"But I didn't know about the faithful servant or iron bars or your piercings when I made the potion! That was a coincidence!"

"Um, piercings?" Geri piped up.

"Yes, he has—"

Noah croaked, cutting off Prim's answer.

Magnolia and Geri exchanged a look, and both grinned. "Oh. Piercings." Geri practically purred.

"Not the point," Prim gritted out.

"It's poetic language," Aspidistra boomed.

Several guests at the ball turned their way.

"It's metaphor and poetry, in its own way," Prim's aunt continued. "It's not literal."

Noah blinked several times.

"Our aunt is right." Magnolia clicked her fingers. "The servant didn't have literal iron bars around his heart. Think of the metaphor. His devotion and love for his master, a nobleman, was caged, or, in other words, unable to be free or expressed."

Prim's eyes stung. "What are you saying?"

"I'm saying his affection and feelings were stifled. The story doesn't even make clear why the prince was cursed by the sorceress. Some versions say the frog was thrown against a wall to transform him."

"No!" Prim shouted, holding Noah close to her chest.

Noah croaked in agreement.

"Don't you dare! Any of you! Don't you even touch him!"

"We won't." Magnolia held up both hands in a sign of peace and calm. "We promise, don't we, Moone women?"

Aggie and Geri immediately agreed.

Aspidistra shot Noah a withering look. "But it did work in that variation of the tale."

Prim dared to glare at her aunt. The temperature in the room dropped to icy but Aspidistra finally rolled her eyes and nodded once.

"Where are you going with your theory of the iron bars as metaphor, Magnolia?" Aspidistra demanded.

"Your heart is racing," Noah whisper-croaked from Prim's hands while Magnolia explained she had an idea.

"I didn't want anyone to hurt you," Prim answered, her voice hoarse.

"You're crying."

"I am!" *She should be listening to Magnolia!* "I'm damn well upset because I did this and I can't fix it!"

Prim looked up through watery eyes to find her family staring. "What?"

A tear rolled down her cheek.

She'd failed. She'd let Noah down, everyone down. Herself down.

More tears fell. She didn't care who saw, what anyone thought. Her default setting these days was teary.

"You know what to do, Prim," Magnolia said quietly.

Prim was about to insist she really had no clue what to do but was cut off from replying as microphone feedback blared through the speakers, and the crowd groaned.

The DJ blew into the microphone and then spoke rapidly.

"Hi everyone, it's only five minutes to midnight and to count down the night of souls, we have special guest band with us on stage, Twisted Nipple!"

Guests whooped and cheered. Some of the witches and warlocks lit smudge sticks while another poured a greenish liquid into a martini glass. Smoke poured over the edges.

Five minutes left and she had no idea what to do.

"But what—*Oof.*" Prim was jostled away from Magnolia and her aunts. Geri was pushed in another direction as the crowd surged forward as the band whipped up the crowd.

"Let's do the mash, everyone!"

Twisted Nipple began the classic hit Monster Mash and the lights faded. Guests were wild, gyrating, dancing, and singing along.

"I've got you," Prim assured Noah. "I won't let anyone—"

"Hey, watch it!" Someone yelled. "Oh, it's *you.*"

Monica scowled, wiping a spill from her drink, and then spied Froggy Noah in her hands. "Why the hell do you have a frog at a ball? You know what, never mind. I don't want to know. You were always witchy and weird in high school and you never changed."

Prim had a rush of blood to her head, fantasizing of bringing her booted heel down on her toes, but ... who cared. Monica was just Monica.

"You haven't changed either, you know. I know it was you behind the prom date prank. I hated you for so long, but now?"

Monica eyed her cautiously. If Noah could forgive her, why couldn't she just get over Monica and her issues?

"You know, now it doesn't matter. I don't hate you. I don't care about whatever this is anymore."

And Prim felt good for the first time in a long time. Looking at Monica now, she felt ... nothing.

She could finally be free of the angst and burden of high school bullies.

"Husband left me three months ago," Monica blurted, her words slurring. "Finally took off the ring tonight."

Prim regarded the Monica's state of her clothes, her make-up. Her dress was stained from spilled drinks. Her hair messy from a big night of dancing, her mascara ran, and there was a tan line where a ring had been worn.

"You're so damn lucky you know," Monica continued, as the band sung about the crypt-kicker five. "You have a bar, and a brewery and ... apples. And—"

"I don't think I'm better than you. Monica, I'm tired of this. It ends here, tonight. The fighting and whatever this is, stops. I forgive you about prom, about the pranks during school. I'm moving on from this. I can't stay in this place with you."

"I ... what?" Monica stumbled but the pressing crowd of dancers only pushed her upright.

"I forgive you. And, I'm sorry about the purple fungus in your locker."

Monica spit her drink. "That was you?"

But Monica didn't get to say another thing as the crowd began to mimic the lead singer on stage and did the twist in the style of a zombie. Monica was pushed and twirled away.

The song faded and the lead singer started a countdown to midnight.

"No. No!" Prim glanced at Noah. "I need more time!"

"It's okay, Primrose," he said. "It will be okay."

"No, it's not!"

A water drop landed on his head and his tongue darted out to wipe it away.

"You're crying, Primrose."

"Because it won't end like the story! I don't know how to break this curse!"

Guests on each side shifted away from Prim and her talking frog.

Someone called her name but she didn't look for who it was.

She kept her gaze fixed on Noah as her tears kept falling.

"I forgive you, Prim."

She gasped, and then hiccoughed. He licked away more tears as they fell on his skin.

"How could you forgive me?"

"Let's count down to midnight!" The lead singer boomed. "From ten, say it with me! Ten! Nine!"

Noah squirmed in her hands. "Kiss me."

"W-what?"

"Do you wish we had had a chance to date?"

"I—."

"Seven!"

"Do you wish we had had a chance?" Noah insisted.

"Yes."

"Six! Five!"

"Do you believe you deserve a chance?"

Right then, Monica lurched into her side. "Oh my god, are you going to kiss a frog?"

"Four! Three!"

Prim didn't look away from Noah.

"Do you?" he asked.

"Two!"

"I'll do it. Wouldn't mind a prince myself—"

"No!"

"One!"

Yes. Prim pressed her lips to the frog and pulled away after a second. "I believe I deserve a chance. I'm sorry."

And then the gymnasium plunged into darkness and everyone cheered and oohed and aahed. Witches and the magical community were not afraid of the dark. They were what thrived in the shadows, after all. Some of the Class of 2004 shrieked and giggled.

Noah let out a sound like he was in pain.

And her arms grew heavy as if she was holding a great burden.

Before she could stop him, Noah jumped from her hands to the floor.

Her cry of *No!* was earsplitting in the gym. Glass vases on the tables shattered. The crowd parted as the table arrangements grew into monstrous creatures, the blossoms snapping their petals like teeth, their stems moving like limbs. Vines rattled against the windows and crept under the doors. Tree outside shook as if they were being wrenched by a tornado, even though the night was clear and still.

"Noah!" she screamed, ready to command every weed, vine and tree to raze the building to the ground to find him and keep him safe.

"We're here," Magnolia said, her hand warm on Prim's back.

Geri looped her arm through Prim's arm. "We've got you, boo."

And then there was light, just in front of her. The crowd scattered to the fringe of the dancefloor. So much light, like a star, like the sun was in the gym in front of her.

Prim and her sisters shielded their eyes from the blinding brightness until suddenly it was gone.

The crowd erupted into cheers and began clapping.

Prim dared to open her eyes as smoke dissipated, and found Noah on the gym floor, naked and very much human and not frog.

She fell to his side. "Noah, are you—"

"Primrose," he coughed, slowly pushing himself up, as the crowd slowly approached.

"Wait." Prim immediately pointed at someone dressed as Dracula near them, who was watching the spectacle. "Your cape, now. Give it to me."

Dracula almost choked himself trying to tug off his cheap polyester cape. She snatched it from his hands and put it around Noah's shoulders.

As she helped him to his feet, the clapping and the cheering intensified.

"I certainly understand the fascination of the iron bar-piercings thing now." Geri fanned herself. "You might want to close up that cape."

Noah smirked as he wrapped the cape around his body, looking ridiculously good draped in cheap black and red polyester.

"How?" Prim rasped.

Noah smiled, and reached up to wipe away the dampness on her cheek. "Your tears."

Prim frowned as Miri bounded up to them, beaming. "Best CovenFest ball entertainment ever! Well done, you!"

She squeezed Prim in a quick hug and then called out for shots, leading twenty people towards the bar.

Music kicked in again. The band covered Sinatra, crooning about giving in to witchcraft, and then morphed into Back-street Boys.

"Dance with me," Noah whispered.

"Why?"

"Because we're on the dancefloor." He leaned in. "And we

can talk while slow dancing. And I never got to dance with you at prom."

"How?" Prim whispered again, relishing his arms around her.

"Dougie said you cried on the roses I gave you. I got side-tracked with my Beauty and the Beast rose metaphor for a few days but it got me thinking. Maybe your tears were the key ingredient for the potion. Tears of rage and anger versus forgiveness." He cradled her cheek with one hand as they danced. "I think you finally forgave yourself tonight."

"Forgiveness!" Magnolia clapped her hands beside them.

Noah and Prim both blinked, having forgotten the world around them.

"My tears? The roses?" Prim said, shaking her head. "You took a chance on a solution that sounds like a Disney movie ending?"

Noah shrugged, smiling.

Magnolia piped up, her eyes sparkling. "Maybe that's what is at the heart of the fairytale. The reason for cursing the frog princess isn't even mentioned. The princess is horrible to the frog and even her father tells her to give the frog a chance, to change her behavior and attitude. She refuses to help a talking frog, acts like a brat. Maybe, the act of kissing the frog is her accepting him and being kind."

Noah stroked Prim's cheek with his thumb. "Whatever it was, it worked."

His voice trembled, half asking, half making a statement.

"I think it did," Prim said, daring to believe. "We broke the spell." And then her face fell. "By the goddess, Magnolia! I need to—"

Noah nodded.

She took a step away from Noah, but he stumbled and Prim reached out to wrap his arm around her shoulder.

Magnolia shook her head. "It's okay. Take Noah home."

"Mags, it's after midnight. I failed—"

"There will other Halloweens. There will be other chances, Primrose Cursebreaker." Prim opened her mouth to argue but Magnolia held up a hand for silence. "I insist." She leant down to Prim's ear. "Give this a chance to grow its own magic."

"But—"

"Prim, it's okay." Magnolia's face was drawn and tired, but sincere. "We will find an answer. Maybe we won't. But I'm okay. Truly."

"But—"

"Prim, you've waited twenty years for this. Go."

"But—"

"It's a year to the day on winter solstice when I lost my powers."

"I know—"

"Then we try that night. One year on. I know we can do it, together."

Prim swallowed hard.

"Prim, go. And be happy."

Magnolia's smile almost broke Prim's heart but Noah's hand closed around hers. She looked up at him and then smiled.

Magnolia took a step back, and then another, shooing them away. "Go. That's an order."

And then she whirled away into the crowd of dancing conference delegates and high school reunion guests.

And Prim knew in that second exactly what she wanted, and needed, right now.

The normie next door.

TWELVE

Away from DJ playlists, cheap alcohol and former classmates in their late thirties thinking they were still young enough to do shots at the bar, Prim drove Noah back to her place.

Noah went inside her farmhouse without questioning why they hadn't gone to his.

"Will I still be able to talk to Dougie?" he asked as Prim pulled out a chocolate stash and leftover chicken schnitzel from the bar.

She placed prosciutto down and whistled for Dougie. "An excellent question."

Dougie flew to the open kitchen window and cocked his head to the side.

"Looks like I'm cured, research buddy." Noah spread his arms wide. "No more frog form."

Dougie made a noise and ruffled his feathers. "Huh, doesn't look like I can understand you anymore. But doesn't mean I can't talk to you."

Dougie cawed and he glanced at Prim. "What did he say?"

"He's pleased you're human again."

"Hmm.

Prim continued to pull more food out of the fridge while Noah moved closer to Dougie who tilted his head again.

"Thanks for your help while I was Frog Noah but, um, guy to demon, I have a favor to ask."

Dougie made a gargling noise.

"Well, can you give me some privacy with your lady of the dark tonight? This is potentially a sock-on-the-door-handle moment here."

"I'm right here, you know."

Noah immediately straightened. "I'm not assuming anything of what tonight means."

She had held his hand and his thigh the entire way home, letting go only to change gears on the truck. She knew exactly what tonight meant for her.

"I think you should assume." Prim pointed to Dougie. "And you do need to give us privacy."

Dougie cackled and flew off into the night.

Was it witchcraft that felt like fate had finally given them this chance to act on their desires? Was it childish to want that to be true?

"You want privacy tonight?"

Prim bit her lip, suddenly coy. "Yes. I don't want a crow watching if I kiss you."

Noah moved closer. "If?"

"I didn't want to presume."

"We've kissed before."

"We have." She took a step closer, letting her hand rest against his chest and she felt his breathing hitch at her touch. "I'm going to kiss you now, Noah."

Her lips lightly brushed his, and then something snapped.

Noah's hands flew to her hips and around to her ass, and

picked her up and placed her on the countertop, inserting his body between her legs.

Their kisses turned urgent and frantic.

Noah broke the kiss first. "So, to check, I'm really a man now? For good?"

Prim grabbed the cape. "You're a real boy now, Pinocchio." She immediately groaned and slapped her forehead. "Shit, I'm making jokes about cursing you. I'm so sorry. I shouldn't—"

But Noah stopped any words Prim thought she was about to say doing what he did so well; he grinned, sparkling eyes, dimples deployed. "You're making jokes and apologizing and curse-breaking all in one night. That's a triple threat, Prim. You're spoiling me."

Prim sighed. "Again, I'm so sorry, Noah—"

"Forgiven."

"Forgiven?"

"That's what I said. I forgive you."

"But how—" Prim huffed. "Why would you even—"

Noah stepped up into her personal space and cupped her cheeks, his Dracula cape well and truly open now but she kept her eyes up, her gaze locked with his. "Primrose Elizabeth Moone."

"I don't have a second name."

Noah grinned broader. "You've been carrying this hurt from high school for twenty years and then had to deal with Monica and her issues for this festival. And I don't hold it against you. I forgive you."

Prim's heart was beating a racket against her ribs. "But why?"

"We're entering our dating era, Primrose, and leaving our high school hang ups era behind us."

"Like a clean slate?"

Noah nodded, his focus on her mouth, his thumbs gently swiping over her jawline.

"Just like that?"

"We're moving on, so we can focus on us." His lips were so close to hers. "Do you want to move on, and date me?"

Prim's breath hitched and she nodded once, that small movement a giant leap forward, feeling lighter, feeling free of the vitriol and regret from a time so long ago. Ew, high school.

"How do we do this? Move on?"

"First, you invite me inside your house." Noah's voice was deep, a hypnotic dream. "And then second, is up to you."

Prim tried to kiss him but Noah pulled back, a muscle in his jaw jumping as he restrained himself.

"I've craved you for twenty years, maybe longer. And I don't want to waste another minute of our lives wondering what this could be. And I know you want this, too."

Prim swallowed hard.

"You made a mistake, Prim, and it's forgiven. All I'm asking if for a chance tonight."

Noah was in her dreams and nightmares and now here, flesh and blood, offering his body, offering a night of lust and longing, and Prim felt like a coward.

"Please, Prim, invite me inside. Let me make you feel good."

She finally nodded, giving in to the ache and took his hand, walking backwards to the front door. This longing for him had a magic in itself as they raced, and giggled, clasping their hands, upstairs to her bedroom.

As soon as Prim's bedroom door slammed behind them, Noah kissed her, and she went up on her toes to kiss him back. His giant hands so gentle around her jaw and cheeks and as soon as she flicked her tongue across his lips, the kiss deepened. Noah had her up against the door in one stride, one hand grabbing her thigh to hold her flush against him.

"But I'm a witch," Prim managed to breathe out in between his fervent kisses. "Doesn't that scare you?"

"What scares me is not talking, not communicating, not being open and honest with each other."

This man. "Then, I should tell you that sometimes, during sex, things can get a little crazy."

Noah cocked an eyebrow. He looked more turned on than wary.

"I'm serious. Losing control during sex can sometimes summon nature."

"Like, vines—" Noah kissed under her earlobe. "And plants —" He nipped her neck and Prim groaned. "And stuff?" He sucked where her neck and shoulder met, grazing his teeth on her skin. "Like you did at the school gym tonight? And the roses blooming?"

She let out a little moan as he nipped her again. "Y-yes."

He paused and cupped her jaw, forcing Prim to look him in the eye. "I'm not afraid of you, Prim, or your magic. I trust you and your powers."

Her heart thudded against my ribs. What magic was this that he could make her heart stop with one little word? *Trust.*

"And I want to fuck you. Be inside you. Make love to you. Give you so much pleasure that I get to watch you come over and over again."

Prim reached for him. Noah was hard, his length pressed against her thigh. He moved his hips into her hand with a groan.

"Is that a yes?" he whispered.

Prim looked down at how her hand slowly stroked him, stalling for time while succumbing to her lust for him. "Your piercings, do they hurt?"

He shook his head vehemently. "They can heighten sex if

done right. We'll take it slow. Find where you're sensitive. What you like."

"Have you done this with someone before?"

He nodded once.

"Good. You know what you're doing, then."

He chuckled softly. "The hardware is new though. I've never been with anyone since getting these new barbells. It's been over a year since, you know, I've slept with anyone."

Noah was offering himself like a gift. Prim was so pleased. Was this love? Having firsts between each other that no one else could have?

Or was being pleased just another form of selfishness? Doubt speared through her. She wanted him for herself. She didn't want anyone else to have this moment.

Noah was oblivious to her crisis. "How do you like to come? Favorite position?" He panted, making quick work of her corset.

"You've already made me come before."

Noah met her gaze; all hungry and dark. "I remember."

"Then you know what—"

"I want to know everything about you, Prim. Every shiver, tremble and gasp."

"Why?"

"Weren't you listening?" he said patiently. "I really like you. And have liked you a long time."

Prim huffed and he kissed her forehead gently. The simple action felt like it might break her with how happy she felt.

She sniffed. "Very well, then. I love oral, to receive and give. If it's penetrative sex, I need clitoral stimulation in order to come and that's best achieved on all fours, with you reaching underneath as you thrust."

Prim cleared her throat and continued. "I like sixty-nine, with women or men. I like dual stimulation, to come together.

I've had anal sex before and it was okay, but not my favorite form of sex. Might have been how it was done, rather than anal sex itself. I like my breasts to be touched. They're sensitive. Sometimes, blindfolds. Not being in control can be a very big turn on, if done right. Maybe restrained."

Noah was a statue, his mouth hanging open as well as his vampire cape. Her corset ribbon hung limply across his fingers. "Fuck," he finally muttered. "You need to get naked immediately."

"Do your piercings make it difficult for me to suck you?"

Noah groaned, giving up on her corset to kiss her deeply. "A little," he breathed against her lips before kissing her again. "Deep throating can hurt and I don't want to hurt you."

"But—"

"Primrose, I'd love your lips around my cock tonight, but we don't have to figure it all out this evening. We have the rest of our lives to explore and do filthy things together."

Her voice cracked. "We've missed so much already. I'm impatient."

Noah titled his head, smiling. "Sweetheart, let me make you feel good."

"No, it's your turn. Let me make you feel good."

She dropped to her knees before him and Noah groaned again. "Please," Prim pleaded. "Let me."

After a beat, he nodded quickly and Prim pushed back the ridiculous cape and there it was. Noah's three piercings on the underside of his penis. Ominous and tempting at once.

She wrapped her fingers around the base of his cock and looked up as her tongue slowly dragged underneath to the tip.

Noah let out a shuddering breath as she flicked her tongue over the first, then the second and then the third piercing. "Does it feel good?"

He huffed out a breath and moaned. "Prim, this is ecstasy."

His enthusiasm gave her confidence to take his tip into her mouth, past his piercings, letting his dick drag along her tongue to softly pop off the end.

Noah fisted his hands at his side as Prim did it again, his eyes fixed on her.

When she sucked him a third time, he groaned a feral sound, and sunk his hands into her hair and guided the pace, testing shallow thrusts in her throat, muttering dirty things about her lips, her tongue, her eyes, her breasts.

Abruptly, Noah withdrew and released my hair. "No more," he grunted.

"But—"

"Not like this. One day, soon, but not tonight."

Prim pouted, giving his cock a squeeze, and Noah groaned again, kissing me and walking her backwards to his bed.

"Are you going to fuck me?" she asked, begged.

Noah swore into her neck, biting and sucking and kissing as we sank into the mattress.

"Condoms," he muttered.

"I'm clean. I haven't been with anyone since, well, for ages. And I use birth control."

"Are you saying it's okay to come inside you without a condom?" His voice was so rough and deep, like his words had been dragged over razor wire and broken glass.

"Yes. I want it. I want you."

"Fuck." He immediately got off the bed and Prim felt bereft, missing his warmth and his touch.

He stood in her room, looking around her collection of dried flowers, feathers, crystals and books.

"What—"

"We need lube," he said over his shoulder, pulling over her wardrobe. "Even though I know you get very wet when I touch you."

Heat pooled down low. Prim was so worked up already.

"Get back here." She reached into her bedside cabinet and pulled out a small bottle of lube.

Noah fist-pumped and he collapsed into bed beside her again, both of them grinning.

"We need to take this slow, so I don't hurt you. Let your body get used to the feeling of my hardware."

She nodded.

"Get on your knees, Primrose."

Prim rolled over so fast she almost face-planted the mattress. She watched over her shoulder as Noah applied the lube to his hand and then fisted his dick, rubbing himself all over, noting how his eyelids fluttered as he swiped his thumb over the tip. How his muscles twitched in his arms as he stroked himself.

"I need you, Noah," Prim ground out. "Hurry."

He grinned, taking his sweet time and it was all she could do not to slap the mattress to make him speed up.

The bed dipped as he kneeled behind and then over her, covering her back. "Spread your legs further," he whispered, and Prim complied, arching her back so that her ass rubbed against his dick.

"That's my girl," he murmured and then straightened, and before Prim could protest, he slid two fingers between her legs and pinched her clit.

She cried out in pleasure as he did it again, conscious she was so wet.

"Fuck, Prim, I'm going to stretch you now." And then his fingers were inside her and she pushed back on his intrusion, loving how he felt inside.

He added a third finger and begged her to sit up on her knees.

With his arm wrapped around Prim's torso, he played with

her pussy and her clit, crooking his fingers when he entered her as his other hand cupped her breasts.

"How does this feel?" Noah panted against her neck. "Talk to me, Prim."

"Incredible," she moaned. "A dream."

He nipped her neck and Prim gasped while he sucked away the sting. "It's real, you and me. It's not a dream, or a spell, or magic. This is just us."

He rolled her nipple between his fingers and Prim trembled. "Noah, I need you inside. Please."

He slammed his fingers inside, angling them again, hitting that bundle of nerves that made everything feel so good. "Right there?"

She nodded sluggishly, trying to move her hips in time with his fingers but it was impossible like this, her back locked against his front. Noah had all the control and that realization made her tremble with need.

"Back on your knees, Prim."

Her arms shook as she obeyed. She was so close already.

Noah nudged the tip of his dick against her entrance and Prim gasped as he pushed himself inside.

His fingers were one thing; his dick was entirely different matter.

Prim moaned as he pulled almost all the way out, and then thrust again, sliding in more this time. So deliciously full, and she could feel those hard ridges of his piercings; not painful but very *there*.

"How is it?" he rasped.

"Good," Prim gritted out.

"It's going to be better than good, my witch," Noah panted. "I'm going to ... thrust now."

Noah pulled out so slowly and then surged inside her, and then held himself still. They both swore, both shuddered, and then Prim realized he was all the way in now, their bodies flush.

He then covered her again, his breath hot on her neck. "I'm going to fuck you now, Prim, if you want me to."

"Yes, please."

Prim tried to push against him but Noah slipped an arm around her waist. "I'm about to blow like a teenager popping his cherry if you do that. I want to make this good for you, Prim."

"It is." To prove her point, she clenched around his length, relishing how she could feel his Jacob's ladder.

Noah groaned into her neck and began to roll his hips while circling two fingers around her clit, making her pant and moan.

"Fuck, you feel so good, Prim."

"I can feel you. The barbells."

"Yeah?" His lips grazed her neck as he sped up. "What does it feel like?"

"It's … good. Very good. More."

He upped his pace again, grunting, and pressed his fingers against her clit, slippery and sensuous.

"No pain?"

"No." Such a little word came out as a long moan as Prim contracted around him and he growled. The ridges of his piercings were lighting up places deep inside she hadn't known were possible nor had experienced before with previous lovers.

"It's so good, don't stop." His piercings also gave her a hint of pain, on the right side of pleasurable. She loved it. "Please, *please* don't stop."

The bed shook as Noah reached for the headboard and rocked into her.

Was the room shuddering? Was the earth moving with us? It felt like Prim's world was literally trembling.

The window pane rattled as vines crept inside the bedroom. The weatherboards, and the house groaned under their twisting strength.

Prim's indoor plants – creepers and vines in hanging baskets and glass bottles – trailed across the floor and then up the side of the mattress and then slid around their wrists, joining them together.

"Oh," Prim murmured, becoming still. "It's happening."

"It's okay, Prim," Noah moaned as vines wrapped around their wrists, binding them. "I like it."

"But—"

"I love it," he growled in her ear, and Prim shuddered, and the vines shook and climbed up their arms as Noah's thrusts built up that exquisite tension. "I'm not afraid. I *want* this, I want *everything* there is with you."

A *pothos* steadily wrapped itself around their waists, effectively tying them together doggy-style.

"I think *pothos* now my favorite indoor plant of all time," Noah panted.

Prim moaned again as Noah's efforts lit up a place deep inside her.

"You're close," he grunted and she nodded. "Did you know that primroses are one of the first flowers to appear at spring?"

"Yes," she huffed, arching her back.

"And ... did you know primrose comes from the Latin word *primus*?" She nodded. "Meaning first?"

"Yes," she whimpered, bucking her hips against him. She was close. *So close.*

"You're going to come first, Prim, and then me," he demanded, harsh and rough against her shoulder. "You're going to come first, Prim,"

"Together," she pleaded, grabbing his hand, their bodies

quaking. The vines were now supporting them, holding their bodies up. "Come with me."

Prim cried out as a wave after wave of pleasure wracked her body, her pussy tensing around his length.

Noah shouted her name, and then bit down on her shoulder as he slammed into her, milking her orgasm as his release took hold of him.

They collapsed, their chests heaving for air as they hit the mattress. Noah was still inside her with two fingers pressed against her clit. Prim had to pull his hand away with a moan, threading her fingers with his, unable to take any more pleasure.

And then Prim realized she couldn't see out the window.

Noah chuckled as the room, and house, groaned as the vines and plants slowly retreated from the window. "You summoned every vine, plant and weed and they covered your house."

"Oh my goddess," she breathed.

"Horny plant witch."

"Bionic titanium dick."

They both burst out laughing. Noah idly made swirling shapes with a finger on her stomach.

"But seriously," she murmured, swallowing hard. "Your piercings heightened sex. That was ..."

He grinned. "Transcendental? Earth shattering? Ruined you for all men on earth, dead, alive or future?"

Prim huffed, and then grinned. "Yes."

She reached for him, and Noah shuddered, pulling her into him and holding on tight. "What is it?" Prim unwrapped herself from his arms. "Are you in pain?"

"No, Prim." He gently pushed her back down beside him. "Quite the opposite." His voice was raspy, hoarse. "I get ... sensations from my piercings for a while after. Sometimes, up to half an hour after sex." His leg twitched as he moaned into Prim arm. "Feel so fucking good right now."

Prim nodded and then pulled him into a kiss, as words would be inadequate.

Noah cleared his voice. "So, those vines wrapping around us."

"Mmm?" Prim looked up languidly where she'd been trailing kisses over his chest.

He shook his head to be able to speak again. "You summoned plants to hold me to you while I fucked you."

She huffed against his chest and then wrapped one leg around his waist and squeezed. "I did. Are you okay?"

Prim hated how needy her voice sounded.

"I am," he sighed, his breath hot against her skin. "And I'm not hexed. And alive. I think your indoor plants like me."

Her mouth twitched.

"And judging by the way you came, I'd say you enjoyed yourself and like me, too."

Prim couldn't hold back her smile any longer.

Noah grinned back, like she'd given him something far greater with a smile than what they'd just done in his bed.

His hand came up to her lips and his thumb traced their shape. "All safe and sound, and in love with the witch next door."

Her breath hitched but Noah's grin didn't waver. "You don't have to say—"

Prim bit his thumb and Noah yelped, still grinning.

"I was about to say before I was rudely interrupted that I'm in love too." She combed her fingers through his hair. His eyes were liquid with tiny pinpricks of stars dancing in their depths. "I'm in love with the normie next door."

EPILOGUE

N oah

"Why, Primrose Moone, I didn't think we had any secrets between us anymore."

Prim froze at the kitchen bench, blinking.

Since Halloween, the last seven weeks had been a whirlwind of dates, kisses on the front porch, and mind-blowing sex using vines as ropes.

And working in the children's ward only thirty minutes away in Wanatchee was turning out to be a great job with a good team and interesting patients.

This normie couldn't be happier.

"But I—" Prim shook her head. "I genuinely have no idea what secret—"

He held up her phone, her music app open.

"Twenty-seven songs in your playlist are none other than Taylor Swift."

Prim's look of shock turned bemused. She tried to take her phone but Noah held it out of reach.

"So, you've got a thing for blonde pop stars as well as metal."

"I will not apologize for having such a phenomenal song-writer and business woman included on my playlist."

"Well, look at that." Noah took her chin gently and tilted her head, making Prim look him in the eye. "Taylor put the rose in your cheeks, Prim."

Prim blustered and huffed, and then he chuckled. "You've got a crush on Taylor."

"I—" Her blush deepened.

"You do." Noah beamed, delighted with this revelation. "My little scion of darkness has a crush on sequins and pop music."

He held her phone up as she jumped to reach it.

"Noah, give it back."

"Not until this has been explored further." He tapped his chin in mock thought. "I would have guessed Midnights or Reputation as your era but your playlist suggests otherwise. You like Lover."

Prim sucked her lips and shrugged, trying desperately not to be affected.

"Sequin leotard, huh? Knee high boots?"

A huff of breath left her lips, her cheeks still so rosy.

Noah relented and let his arm drop. As she reached for her phone, he snagged her around her waist, pulling her against him.

"I had this mad fantasy when I discovered your playlist."

"Oh?" She raised a brow, her face neutral. *Oh sweetheart, you try to look unaffected but those pink cheeks give you away.*

"Could you imagine me taking you from behind, kissing your neck, your shoulders, while you're kissing Taylor and touching her while she touches you?"

Prim's exhalation came out as a breathy moan.

"Maybe I could dress up one night. Blonde wig, sequins.

"W-what?" she breathed.

"Role play idea."

Prim's eyes open and shut languidly, unfocussed like she was imagining the scene in her head. Noah was only happy to oblige with more description. "Imagine me spreading your legs, about to eat you out, wearing the blonde wig and leotard so every time you looked down, you can fantasize it's your muso crush using your thighs as earmuffs."

"She doesn't have tattoos up her arms," Prim argued.

Noah grinned "So when I wrap my arms around your thighs to hold you down, you'll see blonde hair between your legs and my tatts and picture both of us feasting on you."

This time, Prim outright groaned, and he kissed her, ready to put the fantasy into action.

Ever since their night tethered together the night of Halloween with her green witch magic, their attraction had only grown. She was the one he thought he'd never have this chance, this out-of-the-world experience with—no, a *supernatural* experience. He had so much to learn from this incredible woman. And every day he found himself wanting to find new ways to make her feel good.

Twice he'd woke up from a nightmare of smoke and colors swirling before his eyes, and a faint feeling of a sharp jarring tingle going down his spine, but instead finding himself lathered in sweat, expecting his joints pop and turned into a frog again.

But it had never happened. Seven weeks no amphibious shapeshifting at all.

She broke the kiss and whispered against his ear. "My cross-dressing frog prince next door."

"That's niche as fuck and I'll take it."

Her phone then buzzed in her hand between us and Prim groaned. "That's my alarm. I have to go."

"But ... what ... it's time? Already?"

Winter solstice. It was still light out in the afternoon but Noah was still a little groggy from sleeping after his twelve hour overnight nursing shift.

"It is. I have to pick up Geri and then Magnolia to go to Pining for You Christmas Tree Farm."

"I thought you were going to try the spell in the orchard?"

"I was but turns out their rare spruce in stock is the exact one that would be excellent for the spell. Last minute change. Aggie is looking after the Christmas rush at Witches Brew."

"Do you think the ritual will work for Mags?"

Prim had been working tirelessly on a spell for winter solstice for weeks based on a paragraph in her father's journals about the rejuvenation qualities of a rare fir tree native to Germany. And Pining for You had not one but two of them in stock, if you liked having a rare fir tree as your Christmas tree.

"I hope so." Prim straightened and Noah reluctantly loosened his grip. "It will. It's been a full revolution of the sun since her powers were lost. Magic likes symmetry and the seasons. Tonight could mean Mag's has her magic block unlocked."

"If anyone can, you will. And when you return triumphant later tonight, I'll be waiting in a blonde wig and sequins to reward you."

Prim's eyes bugged out comically. "You already went and bought the outfit?" she hissed, worried his father might hear in the next room.

"I did. Express shipping. Arrived when I got home."

"I'll see you and Ray at Witches Brew after our ritual?"

"Absolutely, my witch next door."

She beamed, and then gathered her small cauldron, some glass vials and a notepad, and left after planting a quick kiss on his lips.

Noah hovered by the kitchen window, content to watch her drive off, still amazed how he'd got here, in love with Primrose Moone, and even more amazed how they'd conquered demons and hurts of the past to be this happy.

Prim fussed about in her truck for a long moment. Noah was about to go check if everything was okay when his phone suddenly beeped.

> Primrose: I love you, my normie next door
>
> Primrose: I forgot to say it before I left. But now you have it in writing

Her truck roared to life and Noah glanced up, grinning, to find her grinning back.

And he knew in that moment that while he'd waited twenty years to share her pleasure, hold her secrets and treasure her trust and love for the last seven weeks, Noah couldn't wait to spend the next twenty years, and more, with Primrose Moone, the witch next door.

THE END

ABOUT THE AUTHOR

Sabrina Duval is a Buffy tragic who likes her vampires and werewolves to crack jokes and be a little morally grey. She lives between Brisbane and thirty-five acres of serenity in the Granite Belt region of Queensland with her family and a fat cattle dog-Kelpie cross. Her local rural fire brigade inspired her to start writing small town romcoms under the name Louisa Duval.

As Louisa, her novels have finaled in the Australian Association of Romance Readers for best banter and dialogue, and Romance Writers of NZ's Koru for Long Romance. She was a part of Queensland Writers Centre's *Adaptable* program to pitch her stories to film and TV producers and came second in Romance Writers of Australia's 2022 Spicy Bites '*Machines*' competition with her short story '*Vintage Love Machines*'. She was also published in Romance Writers of Australia's 2021 Sweet Treats '*Chocolate*' Anthology with her short story '*Chocolate and Orange*'. The anthology won the Australian Romance Readers Association's Members Choice Award for Favorite Romance Anthology in 2021.

Louisa and Sabrina send a monthly newsletter with bonus editions with bookish news and latest releases. Sign up to the newsletter using the QR code below and follow Sabrina on Instagram (@sabrinaduvalwriter)

www.ingramcontent.com/pod-product-compliance
Lightning Source LLC
Chambersburg PA
CBHW021924170626
46807CB00007B/2974

* 9 7 8 1 7 6 4 2 3 1 1 1 4 *